A LOVING HEART FOR THE LOYAL DEPUTY

BEAR CREEK BRIDES BOOK 6

AMELIA ROSE

This book is dedicated to all of my faithful readers, without whom I would be nothing. I thank you for the support, reviews, love, and friendship you have shown me as we have gone through this journey together. I am truly blessed to have such a wonderful readership.

CHAPTER 1

"Happy birthday to the best deputy a sheriff could ever ask for," boomed Sheriff Jacob Benning as he raised a toast to Tanner Williams. They were all drinking coffee after another long day patrolling the small town of Bear Creek, their tin cups raised in the air as they celebrated a major milestone for Tanner.

"Thank you, Boss. You make me feel like one of the family, and never treated me differently," Tanner said as they all took sips of their coffee before setting them back down on the table.

"You've always been a good-hearted man, Tanner," said Mrs. Benning. She had her eyes focused on little Katelyn as she toddled around the room, grabbing onto the backs of the chairs and taking small steps to reach her father.

"Thank you, Mrs. Benning. I can say the same thing for Jacob ever since you two got married," Tanner quipped.

"Hey now, I'll take back everything I just said if we start

playing this game," Jacob said as he pointed his finger at Tanner. The smile on his lips told Tanner his boss was just messing with him.

"Fine, fine," Tanner said as he raised his hands to surrender. "Let's just enjoy this beautiful chocolate cake. Mrs. Benning, I still can't believe you made this beautiful dessert all by yourself."

"Ah, it was nothing," she said, blushing a bit as she cut the cake and served it on wooden plates.

Tanner cut into his cake with the tin fork and placed the delicacy in his mouth, moaning a bit at the wonderful taste. Chocolate was such a rare commodity in Bear Creek, it being so remote and the stagecoach only coming through once a week, that being able to enjoy it now was probably the best birthday present he'd ever received. It was sure a grand way to celebrate his thirtieth birthday.

Tanner could hardly believe he was turning thirty. He felt as though he'd just turned twenty and was starting his life's work, with Jacob, as his deputy. It was hard to believe he'd been in the position for a decade now, and he surely never thought about doing anything else. They'd been through a lot together, he and Jacob. Between bank robbers, skirmishes, thieves, and even a sudden sickness that threatened to wipe them all out, Tanner had always worked hard. He was someone Jacob could rely on when the going got tough.

In return, Jacob really had made Tanner feel like a member of his own family. He often invited Tanner to dinner, which was a real treat since Mrs. Benning was such a wonderful cook. Having been raised in Boston and taught to take care of a wealthy family, Mrs. Benning certainly had a lot of cooking skills that the whole town appreciated. She often helped Mrs. Tibet at the inn prepare breakfast and dinner for the guests and other people in town who just wanted something special to eat. She'd made wonderful desserts and often showed Mrs. Tibet new dinner ideas that could be made with the simple ingredients they had access to in Bear Creek.

What made Mrs. Benning extra special was that she was Jacob's mail-order bride. The sheriff had posted an ad in the papers back east, advertising that he was looking for a wife. Tanner smiled as he ate his cake, remembering trying to help Jacob choose one of the letters to reply to. He'd even reread the ones that Jacob tossed in the trash bin just to help him make a decision. But Tanner had agreed that most of the women just wanted to know more about Jacob being a sheriff, and not who he was as a person.

Now that Tanner was older and moving on in life, he desperately wanted to share his life with someone special. He had plenty of friends, but he'd watched most of them marry in the last five years. Even Brown Bear, the Indian chief who was much older than Tanner, was going to be married this summer. It all made him feel that now was the point in his life where he needed to start thinking more about marrying and less about how accurate he was with his pistol. After all, they'd had a few close encounters with outlaws that made Tanner feel as though he was lucky to still be alive. There was nothing like a brush with death to make a man think about his life and future.

"Tanner, I wanted to talk to you about something," Jacob said, pulling Tanner out of his deep thoughts of reflection. Tanner nodded as he set his half-eaten plate of cake down and turned his attention on the sheriff. "I got a telegram from the marshal up in Great Falls. He's wanting all the sheriffs in the territory to get together to talk about some serious trouble that's been plaguing Montana."

Tanner certainly didn't like the sound of this. If the marshal was requesting everyone, then that meant this was absolutely serious. "When does he want everyone to make it up to Great Falls?" Tanner asked.

"In a week," Jacob explained, a hard frown on his face.

"But that's how long it will take people to reach Great Falls," Tanner reasoned.

"That's why we're leaving in the morning," Jacob said. Tanner's stomach sank. He hadn't been expecting to take any sort of trips out of town and didn't quite feel prepared. However, that was part of his job. He had to be willing to act as soon as he learned of what to do.

"Who you going to have watch over things while we're gone?" Tanner asked.

"Mayor Franklin said he'd get a message to Brown Bear earlier this morning when I first got the telegram. The chief should be able to handle keeping a close eye on the town while we're away, and Rosa said she'd keep an eye on your chickens and pigs," Jacob explained.

"Ah, that's mighty kind of you, Mrs. Benning. But I'll leave a note for Curtis to look after the chores for me. He owes me anyways after our last round of poker at the boarding house, and I think this will be a good exchange. That, and he's been eyeing my pigs for a while," Tanner said with a chuckle.

"Whatever you think is best," Mrs. Benning replied. "But I don't want to hear any complaining when you come home and find out that the town's butcher made good work of one of your pigs."

"Wouldn't be the first time, Mrs. Benning. Curtis does make some fine bacon." Tanner quickly ate the rest of his cake, thinking he should get home and pack what he needed for the trip up north. He'd never been to Great Falls before and thought this could be a rather enjoyable experience.

"Well, folks, I appreciate the fine food and dessert, but if we're leaving first thing tomorrow, I best head home and get ready," Tanner said as he stood from the table and quickly gathered all the dessert plates to put in the sink for Mrs. Benning. He always tried to be a good guest and clean up after himself.

"I appreciate your hard work and dedication, Tanner. You'd make a fine sheriff one day," Jacob said as he walked Tanner to the door.

"Thank you, Jacob. I've always appreciated you too, and I'm glad to see you as sheriff for as long as I live," Tanner said with a chuckle. "I'm just happy to serve with you." The men shook hands before Tanner opened the door and took the stairs down to the sheriff's office. He made his way out of the dark space, having memorized it a long time ago. As he stepped out onto the front porch, he made sure to lock the door behind him with the set of keys he had.

Tanner made quick work of mounting his gelding that had been hitched to the post right out front and rode out of town aways to his own modest home. It was a one-story log cabin he'd built after the first year of working as Jacob's deputy. He'd saved up all his money to afford to hire some help to get the job done. It had taken quite a bit of lumber, which he'd collected from the local forest that dotted the ever-looming mountains that surrounded one side of Bear Creek. It had been a lot of work and had taken almost a year to finish, but now that he had his simple home he felt settled and at peace. Or he had, until he started thinking about how a nice woman would be the perfect way to complete the picture.

Once his horse was settled in a stall in the small stable, having been fed and brushed down, and the saddle put away for the night, Tanner made his way inside. He lit the candle at the door and used it to see all the way back to his room. There, he lit a second candle and got out his traveling pack, filling it with clean clothes and his few hygiene essentials. He packed his wool blanket on top, thinking they probably wouldn't be staying at inns along the way. The fastest way to Great Falls wasn't really by road, but by old riding trails that would force them to sleep under the stars. Even with it being late spring, the nights could suddenly turn chilly.

About half an hour later Tanner finally felt that he was all packed and ready to go. His traveling pack was sitting by the front door, and in the morning he'd fill his horse's saddle bags with plenty of food for the trip for the both of them. He'd be able to get fresh supplies in the towns they passed, or in Great Falls itself; as one of the major towns in the Montana territory, he was sure to have plenty of selection for once. It would surely be a lot different from Bear Creek in that regard.

Once he'd readied for bed and blew out the candles in his room, he got settled in his large bed and stretched out as he saw fit. It was perhaps one of the very few things he could enjoy as a bachelor. He had the whole bed to himself and could stretch out after a long day. But that didn't fill the void he felt inside of him. He would have preferred to cuddle up next to a woman he would call his wife. Perhaps even make room for their little ones on dark and stormy nights, when he'd tell them fairy tales and about why thunder was so loud.

Tanner smiled in the darkness as he conjured to his mind all sorts of different thoughts about being married. He tried to picture his ideal woman in his mind but found that he didn't really have a preference. He simply wanted someone he could love and respect, someone who was kind but also brave. Tanner could be called away from home at any moment to assist the sheriff, and he needed a wife that could be independent and resilient for when those situations happened.

The more Tanner thought about married life, the more he thought about how he might go about meeting a young lady that could be his wife. There were no single young ladies in town that he could think of, since most of the female population consisted of children and older married women. There were only a handful of young wives, and that was because they were mail-order brides. He supposed that there were plenty of Indian maidens of marrying age from the local Sioux tribe, but his deep fear of Indians prevented him from going anywhere near the camp in the mountains.

Before Tanner could follow that dark thought to its origins, he rolled over and closed his eyes. He forced himself to stay positive, to think only of what his married life would be like once he was able to marry. And as he kept those thoughts in his mind, blocking out the past, he was able to eventually fall asleep.

CHAPTER 2

Bethany Duncan was sitting in the drawing room of Mr. Bradly's lavish plantation house in Tennessee. She was having tea with Mrs. Bradly and her two daughters, along with a handful of other young ladies from the bustling town of Chattanooga. It was customary for the women to have tea at the Bradly plantation on Tuesdays, when Mr. Bradly would invite all his gentlemen friends over for cards before dinner. This way, any eligible young gentleman who was interested in being married could happen upon the eligible young ladies. And thus was the way of the town's elite business class.

The last thing Bethany wanted to be doing at that moment was having tea in the sitting room with Mrs. Bradly. She'd rather be at home, enjoying a good novel or trying her hand at painting. Perhaps she would take a stroll through the local gardens to enjoy the spring blooms. Or she could take the trolly to the downtown area and window shop. But none of what she wanted to do had anything to do with tea or being seen by eligible gentlemen. The last thing on her mind was marriage.

"Miss Duncan, how lovely you look today in your lavender gown," Mrs. Bradly complimented, pulling Bethany out of her deep thoughts.

"Thank you, Mrs. Bradly," Bethany replied. "It is one of my newer gowns that Father insisted I get for the spring season."

"With your blonde hair and bright blue eyes, you are a beauty that will be easily noticed by others," Mrs. Bradly said, glancing towards the card tables on the other side of the room. Plumes of smoke rose up from the card table, as most of the gentlemen smoked cigars made from the tobacco leaves that were grown on Mr. Bradly's plantation. The smell greatly irritated Bethany's nose, and she tried her best not to scrunch up her face at the smell.

Bethany simply smiled in response to Mrs. Bradly's compliment as she took another sip of her tea before enjoying a strawberry tart. She tried to make light conversation with the other young ladies present, but they were all too busy keeping a straight posture or trying to catch the eyes of one of the gentlemen.

Amongst the card players was her own father, widowed after Bethany's birth. He'd never remarried, which Bethany thought was odd. With his large fortune, it wouldn't be hard for him to find a wife willing to marry even him. Though popular with the elite crowd, Bethany knew the true version of her father and found him to be a cruel master. He was the only reason she was there in her grand new gown and white gloves, her hair curled and pinned to the top of her head, allowing the curls to frame her face. A white feather stuck out from her updo, reflecting the latest fashion. And deep down inside, Bethany hated it all.

Yet there was nothing she could do about it. After all, her father was a very wealthy and powerful businessman with a whole gang of men at his disposal to do his bidding. Bethany alone had three maids, each tasked with making sure Bethany was pristine at all times so as not to bring embarrassment upon her father.

Lately her father had been hosting more dinner parties in an attempt to make a good match for her. At twenty years of age, marrying was the last thing Bethany wanted, while it was the only thing her father talked to her about. He made it clear that she was to marry a wealthy gentleman, and to do so as quickly as possible.

Sometimes Bethany would allow herself to dream about the type of man she would enjoy marrying. He wouldn't be a businessman at all, but someone who was hardworking and did a job that she could be proud of. He would be more concerned about his family than the amount of money he had in the bank. He would have friends with similar values, and when they would get together with other families, she would actually enjoy the company of the other women instead of dreading being around women who only married for wealth instead of love.

"Have you heard about the opera performance being conducted at the music hall?" one of Mrs. Bradly's daughters asked. "I do hope someone will ask me to the performance." Her voice was raised a bit high, no doubt meant to be heard by the gentlemen at the card table. But all the men seemed more focused on the game, their cigars, or the light banter that flowed around each player. Bethany was convinced that this was a complete waste of her time, not only because she wasn't marriage-minded, but because none of the gentlemen appeared to be at all interested in the women. They instead seemed only to care about how much money they could win at the card table.

"I agree that it shall be a very lovely performance," Mrs. Bradly answered her daughter when none of the other women seemed inclined to do so. "I shall take both you and your sister—in lovely gowns, of course—to be seen at the opera." That idea seemed to spark life in the women as they then started to speak about music and fashion. Bethany did all she could not to roll her eyes or sigh too loudly as she finished her strawberry tart, careful not to stain her new gloves.

If Bethany could have things her way, she would only wear cotton gowns, the material being far more breathable than silk or satin. They would be plain in color, meant for exploring the garden instead of being noticed by others. She would learn to horseback ride under the sun and enjoy the sport for the entire day, no longer caring if she became tanned. If her time were truly her own, Bethany would learn to cook all sorts of things instead of relying on a cook or maid to do something for her. And, to her heart's delight, she would grow a garden full of ripe and plump vegetables. Her hard work would be something she could be proud of, something she could enjoy with the whole family.

Instead, Bethany was forced to attend tea parties. The only enjoyment she would be allowed was to be found in either reading or painting, because that's what sophisticated young ladies did in their spare time. She was to be present for all meals, to receive further instruction from her father. And she was never to leave the house unless she had her father's approval and an escort. Her father was so overbearing that he seemed to control every aspect of her life, from what she wore to who she could socialize with.

"There will be a ball in a fortnight," one of the young ladies mentioned happily. "I think it will be the loveliest of events. Everyone will no doubt attend in their finest."

"Oh, what a lovely idea! Balls are so rare that I think it will be the social gathering of the year," another enthused.

If there was one thing that Bethany hated above all the rest, it was having to attend balls. She had to wear her finest and have her hair done up, which sometimes took over an hour to accomplish. Then, she would stand around waiting for someone to ask her to dance, only to discover that she was a very poor dancer. She would yearn to eat the food that was put out for the guests, but her father would forbid it, saying she couldn't possibly risk ruining her gown. Therefore, she would become fatigued easily and end up hating the entire night.

Bethany was starting to contemplate different ways she could get out of having to attend the ball. She could pretend she was sick and try to convince her maids to play along. Her father would attend the ball on his own to make an appearance, and she would happily stay in bed all night reading whatever she wanted and eating sweets until she actually did feel sick.

All of these thoughts were disturbed when the gentlemen seemed to have come to an end to their card game and were standing from the card table. Bethany quickly finished her tea and prepared to leave with her father. When he gestured for her to come near, she stood slowly, smoothing out her gown before gliding gracefully to his side.

"Bethany, I would like you to meet Mr. Spark. He's the owner of Spark Enterprises here in Tennessee," her father explained.

"Pleased to make your acquaintance, Mr. Spark," Bethany said as she dipped her head towards him. She didn't mean those words, but knew that it was the right thing to say. As she looked back up at the man, she could only guess that he was twice her age, and by the size of his large belly, she could also guess he was a very wealthy man that liked to indulge himself.

"The pleasure is all mine, Miss Duncan," he replied. "Your father has told me so much about you already. I felt I couldn't pass up the opportunity to meet you in person." Bethany simply smiled in response, hoping her father would announce that they could finally leave this horrible situation and she could return to the sanctuary of her bedroom.

"Bethany will be attending the opera tomorrow night. Perhaps you would care to join us, Mr. Spark?" her father suggested. Bethany paled at the idea, but kept a thin smile on her face nonetheless. She didn't want to give her father an excuse to lecture her later.

"Why, I would be delighted," Mr. Spark said enthusiastically. "It will be a performance I will greatly look forward to, knowing I get to spend the evening with such a beautiful creature." Bethany knew it was supposed to be a great compliment, so she forced her smile a little bit larger without showing she was straining to do so.

"Well, then. Until tomorrow evening," Mr. Duncan said as

he took Bethany by the arm and led her slowly from the room. As they bid everyone farewell, thanking the hosts for a wonderful afternoon, Mr. Duncan finally made his way out of the house and towards the waiting carriage. He dropped her arm at the carriage door, stepping up into the vehicle first before the footman was ordered to help Bethany up. With a tap of his knuckles on the side of the carriage, the driver flicked the reins and sent the team of four horses galloping down the lane towards the main road.

"What arrogance," Mr. Duncan said as he pulled off his gloves and slapped them against his knee. Bethany jumped, worried that he was upset with something she had said. "If Mr. Bradly thinks he can get a piece of the Remington lands from me, he has another think coming."

Bethany sighed with relief as she realized that she was not the focus of his anger. She turned her gaze out the window to watch the passing scenery and to pretend that she wasn't even there as her father rambled on about business matters that did not concern her at all. She hated when he got into one of these moods and hoped to avoid him for the rest of the day.

The moment they arrived back at the Duncan manor, an estate that had been in the family for three generations, she was happy when her father quickly alighted from the carriage and went inside without saying another word to her. Bethany took her time making it inside the house and walking straight to her bedroom on the second floor. She didn't even bother summoning her maids as she took her time undoing her hair once her gloves were put away.

Once her hair was free from the uncomfortable updo, she changed into a simple day gown before sitting down on her bed and reaching for a novel she would actually enjoy. With the door locked, she didn't have to worry about being disturbed. If her father came to call on her, she would simply say that she was resting after an exhausting afternoon. And if her father really was upset, as he seemed to be, she wouldn't see him for the rest of the night. He'd take his dinner in his study as he thought up a plan to get rid of whatever bothered him.

Bethany sighed as she looked up from her book and gazed around her room. She felt like a bird stuck in a beautiful cage made of silver and diamonds. Anyone who saw Bethany would say that she had everything a person could want in life. She obviously didn't have a care in the world because of her father's wealth. But what people didn't understand was that she was trapped at home under the rule of her father, and she longed to be free. She knew that when she married, as her father wished, she would no doubt be ruled by another master. She wasn't sure how she would ever escape her dreadful fate. But she would need to think of something quickly.

CHAPTER 3

The ride to Great Falls had sure been a pleasant one for Tanner and Jacob. They didn't come across any trouble with the people they passed on the main roads, nor did they encounter any dangerous wildlife when they left the roads and took the less traveled trails towards the big town. The nights were warm, so Tanner hardly needed to wrap up in his wool blanket as they made camp on the ground. With the plentiful conversation and humorous banter between the two, Tanner had to admit that this was probably the best trip he'd ever been on.

As planned, it took them about a week to reach Great Falls. Tanner could see the town in the distance, train tracks dotting the horizon. With this town being one of the main depots for the train heading west, he wasn't too surprised by the size of the town. What really surprised him the most was the sheer amount of people that seemed to be out and about as they trotted into town on their horses.

"First time to a big town?" Jacob asked, a grin on his face as he noticed Tanner's reaction to it all.

"You bet," Tanner replied as he looked all around him. He couldn't believe the number of shops that lined the main road, or the amount of people walking up and down the boardwalk, either in a hurry or stopping to talk to others. Bear Creek was such a small town that he was blown away by Great Falls.

The sound of the train whistle caught Tanner's attention. It cut straight through the middle of the town, making it an ideal place for people to come and go. There were two restaurants on either side of the train depot for both locals and train passengers. Having never seen a train in person, Tanner was fascinated by the large metal machine that blew plumes of steam from the tall, black stack.

"This way," Jacob called over the commotion. Tanner focused his eyes on Jacob and followed him around the bend in the road. He saw a large sign with the word 'Marshal' painted in yellow hanging over a building. There were several horses already tethered out front, and Tanner could only assume the other sheriffs had arrived and were all meeting inside.

As soon as their horses were hitched to the post, they headed inside as well. Jacob removed his Stetson from his head, holding it in his hand as they passed through the open door. The other men that were already inside turned to see who had come in, and a few of them greeted Jacob as though they were old friends. Tanner hadn't traveled Montana as much as Jacob, who often had to see to official sheriff business, so he watched his friend closely, following the other man's lead.

"There's the sheriff," the marshal joked as he stood and shook Jacob's hand.

"Nice to see you, Will. This is my deputy, Tanner," Jacob introduced. Tanner shook the man's hand as well, seeing an aging face looking back at him. Despite the man's age, his handshake was strong and hardy.

"Pleased to meet you, Tanner. Thanks for coming all this way to meet with us," the marshal said as he gestured towards two empty chairs. Jacob and Tanner sat down and talked with a few others while they waited a bit longer. A few more men joined them after a while, and when the marshal seemed satisfied, he whistled loudly to get everyone's attention.

"Welcome peacekeepers of the territory of Montana," Will said loudly, to which everyone in attendance clapped. "I have some very sensitive information I wanted to share with you all that I felt wasn't appropriate for sending over the wire.

"The lower half of Montana is being plagued by a group of outlaws that have no respect for the law. They've been stealing and pillaging, killing anyone who gets in their way. It's a large group, maybe thirty or more men who have banded together to cause havoc and do as they please. And the word I've received is that at least half of them are Indians."

There was a lot of murmuring at the mention of Indians. Tanner shivered despite the warmth of the marshal's office. He had never been fond of Indians and couldn't seem to break the uneasiness he felt around them.

"I need you all to gather what supplies you might need while you're here in Great Falls. You need to return to your homes and towns with the intent to do all you can to protect the settlers of Montana. I have sent a telegram to the nearest military camp with the hopes of having a cavalry unit dispatched to take care of these outlaws," Will explained further.

Tanner could hardly believe his ears. He didn't think he and Jacob had faced anything quite so serious before. And as Tanner looked around the room, he could see the fear on many of the sheriffs' faces.

The next hour was spent discussing the best way to protect townspeople if and when the outlaws made it further up into Montana. Many were hoping that the criminals would make their way to another territory and leave the good people of Montana alone. But others reasoned that that wouldn't really solve their problem. Many believed that it would be best to gather as many people to the center of each town and put up defenses along the perimeter. But as Tanner thought about all the people of Bear Creek that managed farms and ranches, he figured that would be a last defense if the outlaws were spotted round about Bear Creek.

"Gentlemen, I thank you all for taking the time to make your way to Great Falls. You are a great asset to Montana and to the people you've sworn to serve. I wish you all a speedy travel home and pray that God will protect each and every one of us as we fight against the lawless," Will said at the conclusion of the meeting. There was a round of applause, but it sounded weak to Tanner. He had a suspicion that the men were all afraid, not quite feeling prepared for this new enemy.

After saying their goodbyes to everyone in the room, Jacob led Tanner from the marshal's office and to their horses. Silently they rode through town towards the local inn, deciding to stay the night before heading back to Bear Creek in the morning. Tanner longed for a decent bed and a bath to wash away the grime from the road. Thankfully the inn they found had a bathhouse connected to the side, where they could rent a bathing tub and plenty of hot water.

Taking the time to settle the horses in the livery stables, get cleaned up, and have a proper meal allowed Tanner the time to think about their situation. By the time he reconvened with Jacob that night, he finally had a few solid ideas on what they could do to defend Bear Creek. As he sat down on one of the twin beds in their room at the inn and faced Jacob on the other, he began to speak his mind.

"Bear Creek is a small, but widespread town, Jacob," Tanner began. "If we gather everyone now and the outlaws never come, that's a lot of men who are losing time on their farms and ranches."

"Go on," Jacob encouraged as he started to pull off his boots and ready for bed.

"We're going to need scouts, Jacob. People to patrol the open prairies to keep a lookout for these outlaws. Once there is an actual threat, we move everyone into town until the outlaws can be taken out or they pass on by," Tanner said.

"It's going to take a lot of people to patrol such a large area," Jacob said as he set his Stetson aside and lay down on his back. "Who do you think we should convince to help us?"

Tanner took a deep breath. He knew who they should talk to. He was nervous about the idea, even though his brain was telling him he had no reason to be afraid.

"You should talk to Brown Bear and explain the situation. Ask him if he can spare any of his warriors to help us keep the town safe," Tanner said, averting his eyes from Jacob as he started to pull off his own boots.

"I'm sure Brown Bear would be willing to help us out. The success of Bear Creek is beneficial to the Sioux. And I'm sure the people can do something for the Sioux in return if we put our heads together," Jacob said as he fluffed the thin pillow underneath his head. The inn window was open, letting in a cool breeze that ruffled Tanner's sandy-brown hair. Like Jacob, Tanner wasn't sure what the people of Bear Creek might be able to do for the Sioux, but he was sure they could think of something.

Quietly, Tanner got ready for bed and extinguished the lantern that hung from a hook above their heads. With the window open, the sounds of Great Falls filled the room. Tanner tried to tune it all out, to not pay attention to the laughter and commotion from the saloon down the road. He was happy to be sleeping in a real bed but found the noise from the larger town distracting as he tried to sleep. Unable to fall into slumber, he started to think about the current situation once more.

The one thing that kept returning to his mind was that this was a great example of why he wanted to get married sooner rather than later. He never knew what he would be up against next, and didn't want to wait much longer to marry and have children. If anything were to happen to him, he'd like to know he'd left a legacy behind him and a future generation to carry on the family name. He couldn't do that without marrying. And he couldn't marry if he didn't meet a woman. Quickly, he hoped.

Tanner knew that the best option for him was to follow in

his friend's footsteps and place an ad for a mail-order bride. He tried to think about what the ad would say, what type of woman he was interested in, and how he would describe himself in return. He knew that the ad had to be less than two sentences long, and that didn't leave a lot of room to really say much. As Tanner thought hard about what he would say to attract his ideal bride, exhaustion finally took over and he drifted off to sleep.

CHAPTER 4

Bethany was on pins and needles as she sat in the music hall listening to the opera singers on the stage. She wasn't familiar with the Italian language, but she thought they sounded lovely. She would have done anything in that moment to switch places with the singer, allowing her voice to fill the music hall and earning the adoration of the viewers. Instead, she felt trapped in her chair as her father sat on one side of her and Mr. Spark on the other.

When Mr. Spark tried to hold her hand during the performance, she quickly tucked her hands in her lap and folded them together. She gripped onto her fingers, trying to remain calm and collected, as though she didn't realize that Mr. Spark wanted to hold her hand. She hoped that her father didn't notice and wouldn't scold her later for refusing the man's advances. Bethany was smart enough to know that her father thought highly of the man and no doubt intended on them marrying.

If there was one thing she was going to do for herself in her life, Bethany was determined to marry for love. She knew her father would try very hard to pair her with a gentleman he thought would be ideal for her, but Bethany would not spend the rest of her life feeling trapped—she had had enough of that already. If she were married to a man she could actually love, Bethany knew she could at least start to enjoy aspects of life that had been denied to her. Like the freedom to make her own choices in life and pursue her own interests.

When the opera was over and everyone in the audience stood to applaud the singers, Bethany felt a moment of relief. She knew that now that the performance was over, she and her father would return to their home and she to the sanctuary of her own room. She was starting to get to the good part in a novel she'd just started and wanted to return home so she could do some late-night reading before going to bed. Tomorrow would be Sunday and she could sleep in, as she would not be expected at the breakfast table so early in the morning. But all of Bethany's ideas for the evening were ruined when Mr. Spark followed them to their carriage and began to make light conversation.

"Wasn't that just the loveliest experience, Miss Duncan?" he asked.

"I enjoyed the opera very much. Thank you for asking," Bethany replied, taking one step closer to the waiting carriage.

"Perhaps I could call on you tomorrow then?" he asked. "We could take a lovely walk down to the park and perhaps have a bite to eat at the café afterwards." Bethany wanted to say something along the lines that she didn't think Mr. Spark did much walking at all, but her father spoke up for her, as usual.

"Bethany would be delighted. One of her maids can serve as an escort for the outing," Mr. Duncan said pointedly. Bethany just pressed her lips together, trying hard not to speak out of line when she doubted she would enjoy the outing at all.

"Splendid. I shall be by during the course of the morning before the heat of the day really sets in," Mr. Spark said as he dipped his head. Bethany unclenched her jaw as the man walked away, finally leaving them be.

"You're doing quite well for yourself," her father said once they were seated in the carriage and it was rolling down the road, pulled by the team of four horses. Bethany was surprised by the compliment. He rarely gave her any. "You at least learned when to hold your tongue and allow me to speak for you."

"Father, I am certain that I have little choice in the matter," Bethany said, trying not to push her luck. "It is either obey or be hounded for half the day by your bellowing voice." Mr. Duncan chuckled, seeming to find her words humorous, missing the disdain she felt as she spoke them.

"Now that you've grown older, you remind me so much of your mother," he said.

Bethany was shocked by the comment, her father never having talked much about her mother. She in turn had learned to stop asking questions about the woman who had given birth to her, thinking there must have been a reason why her father never broached the subject. Perhaps he was simply too heart-broken over her loss to be able to say anything.

"In what way?" Bethany dared to ask.

"She, too, in time, learned to be obedient. She was rather stubborn when we were first married, but I was able to manage her well after a short while," Mr. Duncan said. The way he said the words made her shiver. She looked hard at her father then, trying to gauge his expression, searching for some sort of clue as to how she should take that statement. But all she could think was that it probably wasn't a good thing, what her mother went through. Bethany's heart hardened more against her father then, and she desperately wanted to return home as soon as possible just to separate herself from him.

Bethany put distance between her and her father as the carriage returned them to their home. She waited for him to step down from the carriage and make it halfway up the walkway before she took the footman's hand to be helped down.

Picking up the hem of her silk gown, she slowly made her way inside. By the time she stepped into the entryway, the door held open by the butler, her father was nowhere in sight. Wanting to keep it that way, she hurried up the stairs to her bedchamber and pulled the servant's cord so her maid would come and help her ready for bed quicker than she could manage.

"How was your evening, miss?" asked her lady's maid as the woman entered and shut the door.

"Lovely, thank you," Bethany said as she was helped out of her gown and readied for bed. Bethany did think that it had been nice to experience the opera, even if her company for the evening was rather unpleasant. She tried to be grateful for the opportunity to see the great musical performance, but she couldn't help but think the only reason she was able to go was because she was being presented to Mr. Spark as a potential wife.

"I brought the paper in for you and left it by your bedside. You might find the scandal pages amusing before you head off to sleep."

"Thank you," Bethany said as she sat and allowed the maid to brush her hair. "I appreciate the gesture." Though Bethany wasn't very fond of the gossip and possible false truths about the prestigious families in the area, she would find the rest of the newspaper very insightful. She rarely had the opportunity to leave the house unless it was to benefit her father in some way, so the newspaper was the only way for her to experience the world outside her bedroom.

When she was finished getting ready for the night, she dismissed her lady's maid, bidding the woman a good night before taking up the newspaper and a candle and settling into bed. With the candle burning on her nightstand, she unfolded the paper before her, sitting cross-legged because no one was watching her to scold her for being so unladylike.

"Seems like Father is really going to have a run for his money," Bethany muttered to herself as she saw an article about how Mr. Bradly planned on increasing his lands for the tobacco fields. She thought it would be a good distraction for her father, that maybe he would be less focused on her for a while.

As Bethany slowly flipped through the paper, distracting her worried mind with various articles, she eventually made it to the *Matrimonial Times*. It was a part of the paper that featured the mail-order bride ads from across the country, in areas where land was abundant but marriageable women were scarce. She sometimes enjoyed reading them, finding them more humorous than the scandal pages.

"A barber seeks a beautiful wife to bare a son to pass down the family business to," she read out loud, trying hard to contain her laughter. It was such an odd thing, but at least the man was being honest.

"Cattle rancher in want of a wife to help take care of the house and kids while away on cattle drives," Bethany read as she shook her head. The last thing she'd want to do is be stuck at home in the middle of nowhere, being left to take care of a whole ranch on her own.

Eventually, Bethany folded up the paper and set it on her dresser before blowing out the candle and crawling into bed. She closed her eyes, thankful for at least a nice home to live in and a comfortable bed to sleep in each night. She didn't like to think about the next day and the odious outing that had been planned for her. The last thing she wanted was to be seen in public with Mr. Spark, but she knew she would have little choice in the matter until she found her own husband and announced their marriage to her father.

As Bethany started pushing all thoughts of Mr. Spark and her father out of her head and instead started thinking about the type of man she would one day like to marry, she couldn't help but think about the mail-order bride ads she had read in the paper. She wondered what it would be like to leave Tennessee behind her and journey west to meet her future husband. She could look forward to seeing the country, learning all sorts of new things, maybe even falling in love with someone of her own choosing. The very idea thrilled her.

However, she wasn't sure if she would ever be able to

escape her father. She knew that if she one day told him that she was leaving and going out west to marry a stranger that he would surely haul her to her room and lock the door, forbidding her to ever leave until she agreed to marry a man of his choosing. Every bone in her body rejected that future, but she didn't know what she could possibly do to escape her current situation.

"I could run away," Bethany whispered into the night air. The very words made her shiver, her body trying to decide if she was afraid or excited by the idea. She was afraid of what her father would do if he ever caught her trying to escape. Or worse, hunting her down wherever she ended up.

But the thought of leaving Tennessee behind, of being able to be on her own and make her own decisions, was something that took her breath away. She could travel by train on her own, make it all the way to where her future husband was waiting, and finally get to be an independent woman. She would meet someone who would respect her, and even encourage her to find her own path in life. It would be a dream come true.

It took Bethany a long time to fall asleep that night, even though she was exhausted from the late musical performance. She was seriously considering replying to one of the mail-order bride ads with the hope of one day escaping her father's house. It would be very risky, but it would be worth the risk to get away from the duty of submitting to her father's will and continuing to live a life she did not want.

CHAPTER 5

Tanner woke early the next morning and got dressed quickly so he could make it down to the telegram office and post his mail-order bride ad. He knew that he couldn't think about it any longer and needed to take action before he started to second-guess himself. He felt that he had the perfect ad put together in his mind and all he had to do was put it down on paper and send it across the wire to the papers in the east.

The sun was barely peeking over the horizon as he pulled on his boots and slipped out the door. He made his way quietly down the hallway and down the stairs to the main room of the inn. Then, he carefully opened and closed the inn door as he stepped out onto the main road and started looking for the telegraph office. Back in Bear Creek, the telegram machine was in Fry's Dry Goods Store. Mr. Fry manned the telegram machine and was always quick to deliver messages that came through.

With Great Falls being such a large and bustling town,

Tanner wasn't surprised when a few dozen people were already up and moving through town to take care of their business. He made his way down the main road, looking left and right for the telegraph office. Eventually he stopped and asked someone who looked friendly enough to point him in the right direction, and he finally found the office.

Inside, he greeted the teller and took the time to fill out the necessary paperwork to send the telegram. He paid a small sum for the message, but thought it was worth the price if the ad meant he would one day in the near future get the opportunity to marry a woman he really cared about. The teller smiled as he read the message, though didn't say a word as he started to tap the key, sending the message over the wire to where it needed to go. As soon as the teller received a reply that the message had been received and would be passed down through the line 'til it reached the newspapers in the east, Tanner thanked the man and made his way back towards the inn.

Tanner wasn't surprised when he found Jacob in the dining room already eating breakfast. They had a big day ahead of them as they started their travels back to Bear Creek. Tanner was looking forward to getting home and returning to his normal routine, though he had a pretty good idea that things wouldn't be returning to normal any time soon, not until someone took out the outlaws that were terrorizing the area.

"Howdy there, partner," Jacob quipped as Tanner sat down across the table from the sheriff.

"Morning, Jacob," Tanner replied as he made himself comfortable. A waitress took his order quickly, which he appreciated since they would need to get back on the road as soon as they got done eating.

"Something catch your interest this morning?" Jacob asked between mouthfuls of pancakes and a lot of syrup.

"Went over to the telegraph office. Decided to place an ad for a mail-order bride," Tanner explained as he took sips from the cup of water on the table. Jacob started to choke on his pancakes and Tanner eyed the sheriff carefully, making sure he was going to be alright.

"You serious?" Jacob asked in a hoarse voice.

"Yeah, Sheriff. I'm serious," Tanner replied with a smile on his face. "All this trouble has me thinking I best get married before I can't marry any more. Don't want to die without leaving this world a few more Williams'."

"My goodness, I've been waiting for this day ever since I married Rosa. Been thinking you ought to place your own ad for a while," Jacob confessed.

"Then why didn't you say anything?"

"Well, because I didn't want you to think it was an order. I was hoping you'd come to the conclusion yourself," Jacob explained.

Tanner nodded, thinking it was a logical enough thing to say. He just thought that Jacob, being as smart as he was, could have thought of something to get the message across to him. But as his breakfast arrived at the table, he decided not to focus so much on it and just have a good meal before hitting the road and having to eat dried meat for the next few days on their journey home.

"You think we'll be needed any extra supplies for Bear Creek?" Tanner asked when they had finished their food. They made their way upstairs to their room to gather their things before they would check out of the inn and head over to the livery stables to collect their horses.

"The people of Bear Creek have always been rather resourceful. I don't think we'll need half the stuff the other sheriffs will be getting and lugging back to their towns. With the Sioux's help, I think we'll be able to manage," Jacob said honestly.

"I just wish we could bring back some of the modern amenities this town has," Tanner said. "Bathhouse, restaurants, a specialty store for almost anything you can think of. You can order a custom saddle, boots, pants, hats. Everything."

"Yeah, it sure is nice and all, but that's what makes Bear Creek so great. We're able to manage without all this extra fancy stuff," Jacob said as they finished gathering their things. They paid the lady at the counter for their meal and stay, and then headed across town to the livery stables. There, they paid the stable hand for taking such great care of their horses and for loading up their saddle bags with plenty of feed for the journey home. Tanner heard some of the stable hands talking about a rodeo that would be coming to town in a few weeks and he thought that sounded like a splendid time.

"Perhaps we could talk to Mayor Franklin about some of these modern improvements for the town," Tanner spoke up as they trotted out of Great Falls. "Might be good to strum up some business and influence some of the farmers and ranchers to come into town more often. Can you imagine hosting a rodeo in Bear Creek and inviting people from all over to participate?"

"You'd have to have a serious amount of money for all the

rewards for the winners to even tempt people to come all the way to Bear Creek. Then you'd have to have a good rodeo stadium for all the events, a place to house all the competitors. It's a big deal," Jacob said as he shook his head. "I just don't know about that." Tanner just chuckled, always able to think up the big plans while Jacob figured out the details.

The two men spent the rest of the day trying to make good time on their way back to Bear Creek. They didn't want to push their horses too hard and risk causing them injury, since it would take a good week to get home.

Tanner knew that Jacob would be missing his family and was anxious to get back, while Tanner wanted to make sure Curtis hadn't butchered all his pigs while he was away. Though Tanner enjoyed Curtis's famous bacon, he didn't want his pigs to be sacrificed for it.

There was another reason Tanner was eager to make good time getting home. Now that he'd sent the telegram for his mail-order bride ad, he was curious to know if he'd have any mail by the time he made it to Bear Creek. It was doubtful, since mail normally took two weeks to travel from coast to coast. But he liked to think he had something more important than just pigs to return to when they reached Bear Creek once more.

CHAPTER 6

Bethany was starting to become rather good at faking illness. First, she had her lady's maid explain to her father that she was having a terrible time with her monthly and shouldn't be disturbed since she was in such pain. That had bought her almost three days of resting in her bed, eating the dishes she enjoyed, and getting to read her novel.

After a few more outings with Mr. Spark, who seemed to be becoming more forward with her with each passing day, even trying to sneak a kiss from her that she found rather appalling, she told her lady's maid to tell her father she was coming down with a cold. This time, her father sent for a physician. After heating her face near a burning candle, she successfully was able to convince the physician as well as her father that she needed to be on bed rest until the cold had passed and she was feeling better.

This time, Bethany had a week in bed to avoid her father

and Mr. Spark, as neither wanted to catch the spring cold from her. When she was finally considered 'recovered,' it was time for the ball. Bethany saw no way to avoid it, since she'd used all her ideas on avoiding Mr. Spark.

The night of the town ball she was expected to dress in her finest and accompany her father to be seen by all the other wealthy families. She secretly hoped that Mr. Spark wouldn't be in attendance.

"I hope you'll be on your best behavior this evening," Mr. Duncan said as they rode together towards the dance hall. "I need everyone in town to see that I am the better man."

"Are you referring to the situation with Mr. Bradly?" she asked, curious to know if anything had developed since she had first learned of her father's problems.

"Yes, indeed," Mr. Duncan said with a scowl. "That weasel of a man thinks he can force my hand by taking his story to the papers. Well, he has decided to go toe to toe with a man who never tires, and never quits."

Bethany didn't comment on her father's words because she knew firsthand that they were true. Her father wasn't one who ever allowed anything to come between him and his business or to get in the way of his ability to grow his wealth further than it honestly needed to be. Bethany wasn't sure just how wealthy her father was, but if he decided to sell all his assets and retire now, he could live comfortably for the rest of his life and never have to worry about business again. Yet she knew that her father was a very proud man and enjoyed not only being wealthy but outsmarting others to gain even more wealth.

As soon as they arrived at the dance hall and greeted the

hosts for the evening, Bethany did her best to slip away from her father's presence. With so many families in attendance, it wasn't hard to step away from her father the moment he started conversing with another man about his current situation with Mr. Bradly.

The first thing Bethany did was find something to eat before her father could scold her. She filled her belly before anyone could really notice her. Then, she made straight for the women's waiting room. Bethany knew she could hide out there for a while since the gentlemen weren't allowed in. She could sit and rest, perhaps converse with someone she knew. But one thing was for sure, she could avoid her father, and Mr. Spark if he was present.

"Did you hear about the unusual business between Mr. Bradly and Mr. Duncan?" asked an older woman as she sat with her friends. "To think that Mr. Bradly would go up against such a man is beyond my understanding."

"Because big dogs like to challenge one another from time to time. How else would they know who would win in a fight?" said another.

"I think the ones who really suffer are the women of the family," scoffed another. "Men focus so much on business and money that the women get neglected in the end."

"With that much money at your disposal, is it really neglect?" asked the first. "If Mr. Duncan was open to remarrying, I'm sure he would have a line of women out this dance hall. Young and old, I know few women who wouldn't mind marrying him just for his money."

Bethany did all she could to refrain from rolling her eyes. She couldn't believe that even in the women's waiting room she couldn't avoid her father. She didn't even want to think about the existence of her father any longer, yet these older women were talking as though his business was the latest story in the scandal pages. Though, she supposed, things could really turn into a scandalous story if her father continued to get heated up about the issue. She knew the type of men her father employed, and he wouldn't hesitate to get rid of Mr. Bradly if the man continued to oppose him.

As Bethany looked around for something to do, she found a corner of the room where there was a seat and table. She made her way in that direction, hoping to avoid everyone present and blend in with the wallpaper. Though she loved to dance, she didn't care to do so if it meant she couldn't remain unseen and avoided by her father. Therefore, she sat in the corner and took up the newspaper, reading it in such a way that the paper would block her face from anyone in the room, or anyone trying to peek into the room and spot her.

Bethany focused her mind on the different articles in the paper. Some of them she found rather funny, though most were dull and boring. There wasn't much in Chattanooga that interested her anymore. She knew her father would not allow her to enjoy most of what the town offered unless it benefited him in some way, so why bother thinking of it at all? He wouldn't risk his daughter being seen in any part of town that society had deemed unfashionable. Her life lacked much of the excitement that she felt other young ladies her age were free to enjoy.

As Bethany started to read the *Matrimonial Times*, she came across an ad that caught her attention. She briefly looked it over, and then paused to read it a second and third time.

"Deputy from Bear Creek, Montana seeks a woman to spend the rest of his life with. Woman must be brave, independent, and find his jokes funny," the ad read.

A smile came to her lips as she thought about the ad and tried to picture the man in her mind. Bethany had to admit that this was the most unique mail-order bride ad she had ever read. So much so that she decided to lay the newspaper down on the table and carefully rip out the ad. Perhaps tomorrow she could write the deputy and start a friendly correspondence. Why shouldn't she have something more to look forward to than her books and newspapers? An exciting correspondence could be just the thing.

"Miss Duncan," said a woman who walked up to her, catching Bethany's attention. "Your father is looking for you."

Bethany smiled even though she was terrified on the inside. She really had hoped to spend the entire night hiding away. But it seemed that her father had grown impatient and had sent someone after her. Bethany quickly tucked the ad into the inside portion of her white gloves. She then stood and thanked the woman before slowly leaving the women's room and venturing back into the ballroom.

Once she was present, both her father and Mr. Spark seemed to come across her at the same time. She smiled to them both when on the inside she felt as though she'd just been caught by a hunter and would now be prepared to be captured. She saw the hard look on her father's face while observing the happy smile on Mr. Spark's.

"Ah, we were wondering what had become of you," Mr. Spark said in a happy voice. "I was hoping you would care to dance with me?"

"Of course," Bethany replied, fearing what her father would say if she refused. But as she felt a sneeze coming on, she quickly raised her hands and sneezed into her gloves. Mr. Spark frowned then, appearing as though Bethany had just done the most disgusting thing ever when she simply could not help it.

"Perhaps when you are feeling better," Mr. Spark said before saying his goodbyes to the both of them.

Before Bethany could say a word, her father ushered her by the elbow out the front doors of the dance hall. She could tell that he was furious, and she silently prayed that she would be able to endure whatever lecture or punishment he deemed necessary.

He didn't say a word all the way to the carriage. The footman and driver seemed to be surprised they were returning so soon but didn't say anything as the driver prepared the horses and the footman hopped down from the driver's seat to open the carriage door. Mr. Duncan practically threw Bethany up into the carriage. She caught herself with her hands and quickly pressed herself into the corner as if she could avoid her father's reach.

"How dare you," he muttered as the door was closed. Mr. Duncan beat his fist against the carriage, signaling that they were to be off in a hurry. Bethany braced herself from the sudden rolling of the carriage, fear in her eyes as she watched her father carefully.

"You have one job in this life, Bethany, and that is to marry well and raise children. You now have a gentleman that is interested in you, one with wealth that surpasses even my own. You should be grateful that I've introduced you to such a man and quickly find ways to coax a proposal out of him," Mr. Duncan rambled, his voice growing louder with each word until he was yelling at her again.

"He is so old, Father. Surely you don't want me with a man like him," Bethany said, trying to express her feelings, to let her father know that she wasn't attracted to the man at all. But Mr. Duncan stilled for a moment, staring at Bethany as though she had a horn growing out of her head. Then he started to laugh madly, which only made Bethany feel worse.

"Child, what does it matter how old he is or what he looks like? Mr. Spark is so wealthy you shall have everything you could ever want. And he actually appears to like you, which is more beneficial for sure. You could probably bend him to your will if you tried to pretend you actually liked him in return. Do you have any idea how many young ladies would love to be in your position?"

Bethany felt sick at the idea. She didn't want to use anyone to get what she wanted. And to think that Mr. Spark would take advantage of her the moment they were married made the sick feeling in her stomach increase. She placed a gloved hand over her mouth, willing herself not to get sick and to make it back to her bed without any further issue.

"I can't believe you decided to hide yourself away for the night. And when I finally convinced someone to go get you, you act as though you are still sick," her father continued. "You've been very disrespectful tonight, Bethany, and I'll be sure to make you remember your error."

Bethany's fear was growing at her father's words. She had no idea what he had in mind for her, but she hoped that she would have enough strength to endure it all. Bethany watched her father push open the carriage door so hard that when it came to a stop it smacked against the side of the carriage, scaring her. She waited until it appeared he was inside before she allowed the footman to help her down. Her hands were shaking, and she was sure the footman would be able to tell.

Slowly, Bethany made her way inside the grand house, constructed of brick and mortar. She was convinced the house would still be standing for years to come, long after she and her father had passed on. It stood now as a testament to her father's wealth and power. A large, cast iron wrap-around porch framed the house, and as she stepped onto the porch and heard the wooden boards give underneath her weight, she stood there and listened to any sound coming from inside the house.

Confident that her father had either retired to his study or gone up to his own room, Bethany entered the house. She looked around to see that most of the candles had been put out for the night. Wishing to avoid further confrontation with her father, she quickly hurried up the stairs in her dance slippers and didn't stop until she was in her room. Bethany didn't even bother ringing for a maid as she got herself out of her ball gown and set it on the back of a chair to be put away in the morning.

It was only once she was taking off her gloves that she remembered the small ad she had placed inside. Setting it on her writing desk, she finished getting ready for bed before taking a candle and setting it down. Once settled at the desk, she pulled out a sheet of writing paper and made sure her writing quill was nice and sharp before pulling out the ink pot. She sat there for a few moments, gathering her thoughts before she addressed the letter to one Tanner Williams of Bear Creek, Montana.

She wrote slowly, making sure all her letters were perfect, and tried to think how she was going to post the letter without her father noticing. She could leave it at the front door with the rest of the letters that were intended to be sent to the post office. But that would be too risky, since her father could easily see her letter on the pile and demand an explanation. If he ever found out that she was writing a man out west, that she wanted to leave Tennessee behind her, she was certain he would go to great lengths to keep her locked up at home until her wedding day was arranged for her.

By the time she finished her simple letter, the candle had burned down considerably. She'd taken her time with each word, and after letting the ink dry, she folded it up small and addressed it properly. All her hope for a better future was encased in that letter.

She hoped that this deputy would find her letter alluring enough that he would reply and they could form some sort of relationship, and quickly. She wasn't sure how much time she had left before her father forced her to marry a man she did not love. All she knew for certain was that she needed to try her best to secure the life she wanted before she had no more chances left.

CHAPTER 7

A few days after Tanner and Jacob had made it back to Bear Creek and filled Mayor Franklin in on what they had learned up at Great Falls, Tanner was ready to put down his foot. Jacob had been trying to convince Tanner to accompany him to the Sioux camp to talk to Brown Bear, but Tanner couldn't even convince himself to do it.

"Jacob, I appreciate you taking me with you to Great Falls when you didn't need to. I know you are showing me great respect by including me more and more. But I just can't go up to the Sioux camp. The idea of being around a bunch of Indians, even though I know they are very friendly and helpful, still causes me to start panicking," Tanner explained. "I will remain in town and help the mayor set up for the town hall meeting tonight."

Jacob placed his hands on his hips and stared down his nose at Tanner. He wanted the man to get over his fear. Especially if these outlaws had rogue Indians fighting for them.

Tanner needed to be able to defend the town against such an attack, not cower in fear when he was one of the best shots in town beside perhaps Emily Roberts. For a woman, she sure knew how to shoot, as Jacob had witnessed last year when the Roberts family had had some troubles of their own.

"Tanner, I'm just worried about you and us going up against these outlaws. I need you to be ready for this. I can't have you go running off when you see Indians," Jacob said, finally coming straight out with the truth.

Tanner looked at Jacob for a hard moment, trying to think of the words that would convince his boss that he wouldn't run away. But the reality was that Tanner wasn't so sure what he would do when faced with an Indian enemy. His fear ran so deep that he wondered if he'd ever be able to conquer it.

"I'll be at the town hall," Tanner said as he left the sheriff's office, not wanting to get in a fight with Jacob. That's the last thing anyone needed to see as they all came together to learn about a new threat to the town. The local officials needed to inspire the people, not give them even more reason to worry.

As Tanner made his way over to the town hall, he kept his eyes open for any suspicious characters. He'd been living in Bear Creek long enough to know everyone. He knew it would be easy for him to spot anyone he didn't recognize. Even with Edward James managing two mines in the mountains, he was still familiar enough with the miners to know who they were.

"Howdy, Tanner," Mayor Franklin greeted as he walked in through the open doors of the town hall. Tanner could hear Mr. Mavis's voice from the front of the building as the teacher finished up his school lessons with all the children.

"Hello, Mayor. How's your day been?" Tanner asked, noticing that Mr. Mavis and his wife were still teaching a dozen Indian children as well. It was their way of teaching the children English and helping the Sioux tribe to acclimate to modern times.

"Good as I can wager, I guess," the mayor said as he placed his hands on his hips. "I've been doing a lot of thinking ever since you boys came back from Great Falls and told me the news. I keep wondering about the best way to approach the problem."

"First is letting everyone know that there is a potential problem. We don't want anyone caught off guard and blaming us for not telling them in the first place," Tanner said as he focused his eyes on the mayor. "Then, Jacob should be back to town as the meeting gets started. He'll have news from Brown Bear, who we all suspect will be willing to lend us a helping hand. With everyone prepared, we'll have enough armed men to protect the town."

"And women, if Emily Roberts has her way about things," Mayor Franklin said with a chuckle. "Ever since she went head to head with the Indian braves and their arrows, she's become a local celebrity." Tanner chuckled, remembering watching the spectacle. The tournament had been brought to town so everyone could witness it as summer gave way to fall. It was very entertaining for many. Yet, it had only made Tanner's heart beat with anxiety.

"Yeah, well. It is all a matter of speculation. If we're lucky, these outlaws will just leave Bear Creek alone," Tanner said with a sigh.

"God willing," the mayor added.

Once Mr. and Mrs. Mavis dismissed the children for the day, Tanner helped Mayor Franklin get all the seating set for the town hall meeting that the mayor had organized. Tanner had even helped with riding out to all the farmers and ranchers to give them a heads up that there would be a meeting and that one member from every family was highly recommended to attend. It was hard to not simply tell everyone the news as he visited with the various families, but instead encourage all to attend that could.

When the pews were all in order and extra chairs had been set up in the back in case there was an overflow, Tanner decided he'd run a few errands before the meeting was planned to start. He figured he could get a few supplies from the dry goods store and go put them away at home before he would be needed back in town for the meeting. He bid the mayor farewell for now and crossed the road towards the general store, which sat on the corner of the road. It also served as a stagecoach depot and the place where everyone came to get their mail or send a telegram.

"Afternoon there, Tanner," called Mr. Fry from the counter as Tanner stepped into the store.

"Hello, Mr. Fry. How are you doing today?" Tanner asked as he walked up to the counter.

"Right as rain," Mr. Fry said happily. "Looking forward to this town hall meeting to learn what all the hype is about. Any chance you can give me a hint?" Tanner chuckled, knowing that Mr. Fry was the town's biggest gossip and would surely send a wave of fear through the town like wildfire if Tanner mentioned anything about the outlaws.

"Sorry, Mr. Fry. I have strict orders to keep my trap shut so everyone can get the same information at the same time," Tanner explained. "But I would like some dried oats and beans if you have any in stock."

"Sure do," Mr. Fry said as he pushed away from the counter while Tanner counted out his change. He set the coins on the counter and took the two small parcels Mr. Fry came back with.

"Oh, before I forget, I know I have some mail for you," Mr. Fry added as he put the change in the till. He bent down and picked up the crate he used to store everyone's mail. Flipping through the letters, he pulled out the ones that were addressed to Tanner. He was surprised to see so many letters and quickly pulled out extra coins to pay for them.

"Thank you, Mr. Fry. I appreciate you letting me know," Tanner said as he handed over the coins and collected the small stack of letters. He tucked them underneath his arm and carried the two parcels out the door and towards his waiting horse that was hitched at the post. With everything tucked away in the saddle bags, he mounted his horse and steered the gelding towards home.

Tanner led his horse at a faster pace than was probably necessary because he was so excited to get home and read his letters. He hadn't expected so many so soon and hoped that one of the letters might be from his future wife. The moment he had his horse settled, he took his dry goods inside and set them on the kitchen counter before sitting down at the small table and setting the stack of letters on top.

One by one, Tanner began to go through all the letters. He took the time to read each one and pay them the upmost respect. After all, these women had written to him with intent and purpose. But as he read them, he felt a big sense of déjà vu wash over him, as though he'd already read many of these letters. And then he remembered where he had. When helping Jacob go through his mail-order bride letters, he'd learned that women often sold themselves short, describing what they were able to do instead of who they really were.

"I'm a beautiful woman who knows how to cook and keep house... about five feet, five inches with knowledge of sewing, mending, and gardening...ready to start a family and be a great wife and mother..."

It was the same thing over and over again. He had no doubt that the women were telling the truth about what they were capable of doing. Tanner simply didn't get a sense of who these women really were as people. Plenty of mail-order brides had come to Bear Creek needing to learn how to survive in a remote town and do things for themselves. As long as a young lady was willing to learn and had a good attitude, then she would surely do well in Bear Creek.

By the time Tanner reached for the last letter, his hopes of finding a wife he might one day fall in love with were quickly dwindling. He'd reread the letters later to determine which one was the best, or perhaps use them for kindling and hope that a better letter eventually came to him. But as he opened the letter addressed to him from Tennessee, he was quickly surprised by not only the beautiful penmanship, but the way the author had written the letter.

Dear Mr. Williams,

I'm writing you late at night after having attended a rather spectacular ball in town. The dance hall had been wonderfully decorated, and the food was particularly yummy. However, even though I've been born into privilege, I would greatly give it all up for a chance to be an independent woman with my own hopes and dreams.

That is why I took your ad from the paper I found at the ball. Now I write to you with the hope of becoming familiar enough with you to come to Bear Creek to escape what I feel like is a bird's cage. My father is rather overbearing, intent on marrying me to the highest bidder, you could say. This is not the type of life I envisioned for myself.

Even though I've been raised all my life with much convenience, I'm not afraid of facing the wilds of the west. I want to learn to ride a horse, cultivate my own garden, and wear gowns that are actually comfortable. I want to be proud of what I can achieve with my hands and strength. And in turn, I want to be proud of my husband. All the men here are businessmen, only focused on fortunes instead of family. I want to marry a man I can respect, who loves his family; someone I can love deeply.

Enclosed is one of my few prized possessions that I can call my own. It was a photo taken of me last year for my father to show his colleagues. He hoped, of course, to spark interest in a wealthy man who would like to marry me and thus create a strong business alliance. I would say it is a close resemblance of what I look like. And I hope this letter details what I am actually like.

Well then, that is all for now. I look forward to your reply if you feel inclined to do so.

Sincerely,

Bethany Duncan

TANNER PICKED up the small photo, never having seen a photo in person before. He'd seen photos printed in the paper from time to time, but they were never as clear as the original. The black and white photo in his hand showed a beautiful young lady in a very fancy gown. A plume feather stuck out of her curly hair, which had been pinned to the top of her head. She wore gloves on her hands, which were folded in her lap. Though there was not a smile on her face, he saw the humor in her eyes. He figured she had light blonde hair and light eyes based on the photo. He could tell that she was very beautiful, indeed. And her letter had been rather captivating. She was honest about her life and her lack of skills. Yet, she had written of a desire to learn.

Tanner knew for certain to whom he would be replying. He left her letter on the table along with her photo. If it was one of her most prized possessions, then he didn't want to risk carrying it around with him and crinkling it. He would leave it there and come home looking forward to seeing the photo, just like he would his future wife.

Once everything was settled at the house, he collected his horse once more and rode back into town. The remote town was bustling with people as families from all over the area came in to listen to what the mayor had to say.

Tanner left his horse hitched at the sheriff's office, thinking the livery stables would be full tonight and any space near the town hall would be filled with horses and carriages. He greeted as many people as he could as he made his way through the crowd, into the building, and towards the front to stand with Mayor Franklin and Sheriff Benning.

"I wondered where you'd run off to," Jacob said with a smile.

"I received some letters and rode home real fast to read them," Tanner explained in a soft voice.

"Oh yeah? Get any good ones?"

"Just one," Tanner said with a smile. "And she included her photo, too."

"You bring it with you?" Jacob asked, sounding excited.

"No, I left it at home. Didn't want to ruin it," Tanner said. "But I'll show you if I get another letter. I plan to reply tonight when I get home."

"You take a sheet of writing paper from the sheriff's office if you need it."

"Thanks, Boss. I appreciate it," Tanner said right before the mayor whistled, gathering everyone's attention. The rest of the people coming into the building quickly found a spot to sit down at or stood at the back as the seats quickly filled. Tanner didn't think this many people would have decided to attend, but he thought it was a good sign. The more people learned about the truth tonight, the quicker everyone could start preparing for the worst possibilities.

"Folks, thank you all for coming into town tonight," the Mayor said over the crowd, speaking as loud as he could for those in the back. "I wouldn't have called you all here tonight if it wasn't absolutely important. I know a lot of you are sowing your fields now that the ground is no longer frozen. So, I'll make this quick and to the point.

"Sheriff Benning and Deputy Williams have just come

back from Great Falls, where they met with the marshal of Montana. They've been warned of a group of outlaws, a band about thirty, who are causing havoc in the lower part of Montana. We have been warned of their trouble, told that these men are pillaging and causing damage wherever they go. They take what they want and destroy everything in their path." A low murmur filled the town hall then, but the mayor did not stop to let the sound grow any louder.

"We want to share the news of these troublemakers with all of you so you can all keep a lookout for a large group of people traveling by your lands or off in the distance. If you see them coming your way, don't wait to see what they want. You get your family together and ride straight into town. Once we know for certain they're crossing paths with us, we'll have everyone relocate to town 'til they can be dealt with."

"Why don't we just move to town now?" called a man from the crowd.

"Bear Creek isn't quite ready for everyone to come on in. The town hall will be cleared of the extra pews and cots will be placed here for when the time comes, if it happens. Preparations are being made, but they are not ready yet."

Before any other question could be asked, Jacob stepped forward and addressed the crowd. "I've spoken with Brown Bear of the Sioux Indians. He has agreed to lend us his braves and warriors to help protect the people of Bear Creek.

"Starting tomorrow, you may see groups of three Indians riding together on ponies. These Indian ponies will have large white circles painted on their rumps so you'll know that they are friendly. They will be patrolling the area to keep an eye out for these outlaws. If you're in trouble and need help, you can call on them for assistance. They're able to speak English and will be armed to protect you."

"How do you know we can trust the Sioux?" called someone from the crowd. "They could just turn on us and use this time to kill us all." There were a few agreements from others that made Tanner worried. The last thing they needed was division amongst the townspeople.

"The Sioux could have come down from the mountain and killed us all a long time ago if they chose," Jacob hollered over the crowd, quieting them instantly. "But instead they have chosen to help us and even protect us. So I'd appreciate it if you focus on the reality of the situation instead of the 'what ifs'. If this band of outlaws makes their way to Bear Creek, they will kill you. That is the reality."

No one said anything bad about the Sioux for the rest of the night. There was much discussion about the preparations that would need to be done in order to prepare for all the local families coming to stay in town if danger did come their way. Farmers and ranchers were encouraged not to engage with any strangers, but to be prepared to abandon their homesteads the moment they suspected any sort of danger. It was all rather grim and foreboding, but Tanner knew it was best to prepare people instead of leaving them vulnerable.

It was late in the evening when the meeting was finally brought to an end. There was much conversation as families slowly made their way from the town hall. Tanner wished he had a better sense of what people were feeling as they left into the darkness and made their way home. He could only assume that many of them were afraid, and Tanner supposed that their fear would help them to remain safe and cautious during their day-to-day lives.

"We'll be seeing you in the morning," Jacob said to Tanner, pulling the deputy out of his deep thoughts.

"Sure thing, Boss," Tanner said with a nod.

"Don't stay up too late writing letters," Jacob quipped as he steered his wife and child from the town hall. Tanner smiled as he watched the family go, thinking he'd like to have a family of his own one day, as soon as all this trouble was behind them.

CHAPTER 8

After the evening of the ball, Bethany was subjected to the strangest punishment her father had ever thought of. Most of the time, she was forced to remain in her room and take meals there so she could think about what she had done wrong. She never minded those punishments, as it gave her more time to read and let her avoid her father. But this time he'd gotten very creative. This time, he thought up a punishment that he thought would make her more respectful of their way of life.

In the early mornings, Bethany would be woken by one of the maids, who would coax her out of bed. She was forced to sleep in the servant's quarters, and she had to rise early and get to work like the rest of them. Bethany was shown how to do laundry, how to cook, and how to maintain the house. She was given plain gowns to wear, matching those of the other maids, and from dawn 'til dusk, she was taught to work like any other servant.

Her father gained much pleasure out of seeing Bethany work for the first time in her life. He would often give her specific orders, telling her to make him a cup of tea, or go fetch the newspaper from the front porch, or go into town to run errands with the rest of the maids, so long as she was well disguised. And though her father assumed she had really started to hate life and yearned to return to her bedchamber and experience the convenience of his wealth, Bethany was actually enjoying life for the first time.

Bethany didn't mind the work, even when it was rather dirty. She found learning new skills to be interesting and worked hard to show the other maids that she was just as capable as they were. She became closer friends with them than she had anyone else and thought her tasks could sometimes be rather fun. She thoroughly enjoyed learning to cook, even when the kitchen became very hot with the wood burning stove, but the joy she felt from successfully baking a pie or roasting a chicken was well worth the effort.

The best part of this punishment was that she was able to accompany the maids into town to run errands. There, she was able to post her letters to Tanner and check with the postmaster to see if any letters had arrived for her. That way her father would never find out that she was exchanging letters with a deputy out west.

"What are you going to do when your father forces you to marry?" Matilda asked. She was the one maid that Bethany had grown close to over the past month of working as a servant. She wasn't sure how long this punishment was going to last, but she hoped it would never end. Bethany felt, for the first time in her life, a sense of pride in her abilities and actions.

"I'm not sure," Bethany said as they folded laundry together, taking the dry items off the clothesline and folding them neatly in the baskets. Even though it was only her and her father in the family, the laundry still needed to be done for all the servants who lived in the house. Bethany hadn't realized just how many servants there were until she had to do all their laundry.

"You could slip away in the middle of the night. Try to outrun your father before he realized you were missing," Matilda suggested.

"And allow the wrath of my father to fall on this house?" Bethany reasoned. "He would have everyone whipped, thinking the servants had let me escape somehow."

"Do you really think he would do such a thing?" Matilda asked as she handed Bethany another shirt from the line. Today Matilda was taking the clothes down while Bethany hurried to fold everything.

"I know my father has a horrible temper," Bethany said. "And there is no saying what he would be capable of doing if I ran away. He'd send out every hired gunman in the state just to hunt me down."

"But it would be rather hard for them to find you if you went as far as Montana," Matilda said. "I doubt they'd be able to find you there. Just think of how well you're able to disguise yourself when we go to run errands together."

Bethany became quiet after that as she thought about what Matilda had just told her. She had become quite good at hiding her identity anytime she needed to go to the shops or groceries to pick up something for Cook. No one ever recognized her, not even Mrs. Bradly, who she'd run into once. Mrs. Bradly had assumed that Bethany was another servant from the Duncan household and had turned her nose up at the same woman she'd so recently hosted at her home. It had been quite a surprising situation and had taught Bethany a lot about appearances.

Later in the day, Bethany sat in her room in the same hallway that housed the other maids, reading over Tanner's latest letter. She had snagged it from the postmaster when she and Matilda had needed to go into town for specific ingredients. Cook was making a special dinner and Bethany could only assume her father was hosting a dinner party that she wouldn't be invited to. But she was perfectly fine with that fact as she read over the letter, smiling to herself.

Dear Bethany,

I hope you don't mind that I'm using your first name. We've exchanged a few letters, and think we are comfortable enough with one another to do so.

Things in Bear Creek have continued as normal. We are taking all the precautions we can in case Bear Creek is threatened by these outlaws. So far, no sign of them. But we aren't going to let our guard down until we receive the official telegram that they've been caught or taken care of.

In the meantime, I've been getting used to seeing a lot more Indians in and around town. The Sioux have been kind enough to lend their strongest warriors. It seems that many of the younger men are eager to see some sort of action, since it is peaceful times for all the Indians. No more do Indian tribes roam the prairies, and the next generation of Indians does not know what it is like to fight in battle. Yet, they are still trained to fight if need be, and are now eager to face these outlaws and be able to tell their own families one day that they fought in a great battle to protect the people of Bear Creek.

I look forward to all of your letters, to hearing about your life in Tennessee. I like to hear about the things you have been learning and find it humorous that you find pride in doing housework. I suppose that's understandable if you've never done it before. I think your positive attitude is wonderful.

Tanner

BETHANY COULDN'T CONTAIN her smile as she read the letter again and again. She enjoyed receiving Tanner's letters and learning about what life was like in Bear Creek. Their troubles were completely different, and she would be the first to say that what Tanner was dealing with was by far worse than her being forced to learn to do housework.

Tanner was right about her trying to keep a positive attitude about things, and she felt he was doing the same thing in Bear Creek. She found the description of the Sioux Indians very interesting and thought Tanner had to be brave to not fear working with them. After all the stories she had heard, she felt that she would be deathly afraid.

When someone started knocking on the door to the small room, Bethany quickly stashed her letter underneath her pillow and stood from the bed. Taking a deep breath, she opened the door to see Matilda was standing on the other side, holding a gorgeous rose gown in her hands.

"Your father has requested that you join him for dinner," she explained, making her way into the room with two other maids. They carried all the things needed to get her ready for the evening. Bethany didn't even bother saying a word as she allowed the maids to do their work. She hadn't worn a fine gown in such a long time that she was surprised by how soft the silk was, and by how refreshing the smell of rose water was on her skin. Perhaps there were a few things she missed about living a life of luxury. Yet, she knew now that she could do without all of that.

Once her hair had been done and her white gloves were on her hands, she left the room and walked all the way across the house towards the dining room. There, she could hear light conversation and figured her father would expect her to be on her best behavior. Perhaps he even expected her to be grateful to attend the dinner party. Did he expect her to plead with him to allow her to return to her old bedchamber? Or could she possibly do something tonight that would allow her to remain in servitude like she preferred?

As she entered the dining room, she kept a simple smile on her face. She made her way to the head of the table and sat next to her father, where her place was in the family. She wasn't at all surprised when she heard murmuring upon her arrival, or when she saw that Mr. Spark sat on her right. After almost a month without being forced to socialize with others, she immediately felt uncomfortable and desperately wished to return to her small room in the servant's quarters.

"Good evening, Bethany. How are you feeling today?" Mr. Duncan asked his daughter.

"Perfectly well, Father. I've had such a splendid day," Bethany said with a bright smile. Mr. Duncan hadn't been expecting such a response and seemed baffled by her words.

"We haven't had the opportunity to dine together in some time," Mr. Spark said, a bright smile on his face. "I have missed your company."

"How do you like the food, Mr. Spark?" Bethany asked. She dearly wanted to say how much she disliked the man and hated his company but figured it would only cause her father to become angrier than he already appeared by her comment.

"Ah, the food here at the Duncan house is always sublime," he said happily, raising his wine glass and drinking quite a bit before setting it back down again. He gestured over his shoulder towards the footman and the servant dutifully filled his glass once more. Bethany had a clear picture of what type of man Mr. Spark was, and she felt sick at the idea of having to marry him one day.

Throughout the dinner, Bethany kept in her mind her letters from Tanner. It was the only way she was going to remain positive throughout the night and keep up with the light conversation around the room. She didn't care for a single person in the room, and therefore imagined what she would say if she was dining with Tanner or the friends he had described to her in his letters. She could easily picture Mr. and Mrs. Benning at the table, or the Jenkins family. They would surely be far better company than she was enduring at that moment.

"Miss Duncan, would you care to accompany me

tomorrow to the Watering Hole? I hear the local band is fabulous and that the food is rather good. We could spend the evening dancing," Mr. Spark said. Bethany was a bit surprised by the invitation. She knew that the Watering Hole was a saloon and was not a place for a proper young lady such as herself. Bethany had to look towards her father for any idea on how she should answer the man.

"Perhaps Smith and Cox would be a better place to dine?" suggested Mr. Duncan. "The food is far better."

"Sure, sure," chuckled Mr. Spark. "But the entertainment is not as enjoyable."

"Then I am sure that Bethany would enjoy herself with you," Mr. Duncan said. "I'll have her lady's maid chaperone for the night."

"No need for a chaperone," Mr. Spark remarked. "We will only be out for a little while. Just long enough to have a pleasant meal and dance a few songs."

Bethany didn't like the sound of what Mr. Spark was implying. First, he was suggesting a scandalous place for them to appear in. And now he wanted her to go without a chaperone? It only made Bethany think that Mr. Spark had other ideas in mind than just going out to eat and dance. It made her very nervous, and she looked towards her father for help. He observed Mr. Spark closely for almost a minute as he chewed his prime rib. Then he looked at Bethany and grinned an evil smile.

"Sure, Mr. Spark. I'm confident you two will have a pleasant night," Mr. Duncan said. Bethany was completely surprised. Did he not care about their reputation? Was he not worried that Mr. Spark was planning something dubious for her?

"Fantastic. I thoroughly look forward to it," Mr. Spark said, daring to wink at her.

For the rest of the dinner, Bethany focused on trying to eat something while her stomach tightened in knots. Afterwards, she stood with her father at the front door as they said good night to all the dinner guests. The moment the last guests were being carted down the road by their carriage, Bethany turned on her father.

"Father, you can't be serious about tomorrow night," she said as the butler shut the front door.

"I'm perfectly content at the thought that Mr. Spark and you will enjoy your evening," Mr. Duncan said as he turned from his daughter and started towards his study.

"But the Watering Hole is not a place for a young, unmarried woman. It's not a place one goes while courting. It's a place for loose women who want something in particular from drunken men," Bethany continued, following after her father. "You can't honestly think it's an appropriate place for Mr. Duncan's daughter."

"Bethany, you will soon be married and no longer my concern. Your reputation will reflect your husband's, not mine," he said as he sat down at his desk. Bethany stood at the doorway of his study, knowing that she had been forbidden to ever enter the room.

"But I am not yet married, Father. That is the point I am trying to make. I should not be allowed anywhere near the Watering Hole. And certainly not without a chaperone," Bethany said, her temper rising.

"This matter is not up for discussion," her father said as he looked up at her, his dark eyes burrowing into hers. "You are dismissed. Tomorrow you shall resume your duties, and in the evening you will prepare for your outing with Mr. Spark."

Bethany could hardly believe what was happening. She stared at her father for a moment longer, wishing she could scream and yell at him as he so often did to her. She wished her screams could convince him to change his mind. But she wouldn't stoop to his level.

She turned instead and hurried to her room in the servant's quarters. She got to the room just as the tears started to flow down her face. As she crumbled onto her bed and tried to use the thin pillow to quiet her sobs, she wished she were in Bear Creek with Tanner. She would rather face Indians and outlaws than be left alone with Mr. Spark in a saloon.

CHAPTER 9

Tanner focused on remaining calm and breathing deeply as he stood on the porch of the sheriff's office and listened to Jacob speak to the five groups of three Indians. They'd been meeting with this group every morning and evening to go over what they were seeing in the distance around Bear Creek. Tanner knew that the Sioux were a vital ally and one that was really helping the people of Bear Creek. But being around so many Indian warriors, bows and arrows strapped over their shoulders, made Tanner very nervous. And he was certain that his nervous stance was noticed by the Indians.

"It's pretty hot today, so make sure to bring plenty of water with you," Jacob said. The Indians chuckled in return.

"Do not worry, Sheriff. We know how to take care of ourselves during the hot days," said an Indian warrior.

"I don't doubt that, but I still want you all taking care of yourselves. I want you to know that I truly care about your well-being. Your service to the people of Bear Creek, and to the territory of Montana, will not be overlooked. Tanner and I are trying to think up something real special to show you all our thanks for your service," Jacob explained.

"Cattle for the winter months," said one warrior.

"Or perhaps a shiny metal badge like you have," said another, causing them all to chuckle. Tanner simply watched the friendly banter with anxious eyes, watching every movement as though it could be a sign of danger.

"We'll have to see about that one," Jacob said through his mirth. "Now you all have a good day, and please send one of your group back if you see anything suspicious. We have to be ready to act the moment these outlaws make their presence known."

"Don't worry, Sheriff. The Sioux will not allow the people of Bear Creek to be slaughtered. If there are bad Indians in this group, it is our duty to put a stop to them," said one of the older Indian warriors. The man's eyes shifted towards Tanner's, and Tanner did all he could not to look away. He managed to blink, but that was all.

When the Indians left town, riding out on their painted ponies, Tanner felt as though he could finally breathe easy again. They'd been going through this routine for over a month now and still Tanner didn't seem to be able to shake the nerves that rose up in him every time he met with the Indian warriors. He'd been trying hard to overcome his fear of them, but still couldn't seem to shake the deep-rooted feelings.

"Still as shaky as ever, Tanner," Jacob observed as they headed back into the sheriff's office. Laid out on the sheriff's desk was a hand-drawn map of the territory of Montana. On it were little notes that contained the information Jacob had received about where the outlaws had been spotted last. To Tanner, it seemed the outlaws were heading straight for Bear Creek.

"I don't know what else to do," Tanner said as he sat down at his desk and ran his hands through his sandy-brown hair.

"You could always go up to camp and live with them for a week. That would surely do the trick," Jacob suggested.

"And if we weren't expecting to see these outlaws any day now, I might actually consider the idea," Tanner replied. "I know the Sioux are our only hope for protecting such a large number of people. I just can't help but look at them and feel a great sense of uneasiness. It has to be all the stories I heard as a kid about Indians and how dangerous they could be to settlers."

"I'm really sorry about what happened to them," Jacob said in a soft voice. "I can't imagine what you must be going through."

"It was a long time ago, Jacob. But something that may haunt me for the rest of my life," Tanner said with a sigh.

"Any letters from Bethany lately?" Jacob asked, figuring he'd change the subject.

"No. But I sent out my last letter not that long ago. Another week or two, I think, before I expect another letter," Tanner explained. Bethany's letters had become a beacon of light in his dark life. At night he would often reread them and look forward to her next one. He found her father's punishment for her amusing, since she seemed to enjoy it so much. He also thought it was fitting for her, if she really wanted to come out west and meet him.

“Well, we better get over to the town hall and see how the preparations are coming along. Mr. Fry has been stocking up on extra food just in case the town gets put into a siege situation by the outlaws. Cots have been put up in every extra space, including the empty store fronts, the town hall, and even the dining room at the inn,” Jacob explained.

“Better safe than sorry,” Tanner reasoned as he took one last look at the map. With what he was able to see, the outlaws were heading straight north, and Bear Creek was right in their path. Tanner prayed at night that they would all be spared, but it was hard to be positive after reading the daily telegrams they received about what was happening to the towns around them.

“Any news from the marshal about his efforts to get a cavalry unit dispatched to Montana?” Tanner asked as he followed the sheriff out of the office and towards the town hall.

“Nothing as of late,” Jacob replied. “Last telegram explained that there are no cavalry units close enough to get here in time.”

The conversation made Tanner think of the cavalry unit that had been sent to Bear Creek a few years back to move the Sioux to a reservation. The Sioux had been able to bribe the cavalry leader into taking a bunch of gold and leaving them alone. It had been Edward James who had really helped out with that plan, but in the end it had worked perfectly.

“It makes me wonder what’s influencing these men to do such terrible things,” Tanner said as he walked alongside Jacob. They passed by several other people, the town having become quite busy in the past weeks. More families were sticking close to town just in case the outlaws made an appearance.

"They must have a reason besides just the pleasure of stealing and killing," Jacob said in a hushed voice. He didn't want to scare anyone they were passing. "And the fact that there are Indians in the mix makes me wonder what's in it for them."

"Revenge, perhaps?" Tanner mused. "A common hatred that they're taking out on innocent people?"

"Regardless of the reason, I just hope we never have to find out why," Jacob said in a serious voice. Tanner observed him, noticing the hard edge in his jaw. He wondered if Jacob was just as nervous as he was about the whole situation. If he was, he was sure hiding it well.

CHAPTER 10

Bethany's heart was pounding in her chest as she rode in the carriage with Mr. Spark. She sat on the opposite side, squishing herself into the corner so she could create as much distance between them as possible. He was smiling at her, staring at her openly, and his gaze made her skin crawl uncomfortably.

"You look lovely this evening," he said, his voice thick. Bethany had dressed in her most modest gown that was still fashionable enough for a lady of her status. There was no neckline at all, the gown coming up to cover her neck. It was a gown more fitting for the colder months, and already she felt rather warm with the high neck and the long sleeves. She'd even worn gloves, because she didn't dare touch Mr. Spark's bare skin if he convinced her to dance with him that night.

Bethany didn't reply to Mr. Spark's compliment but instead kept her eyes on him the entire ride to the Watering Hole. She watched his every movement as though she was a mouse and he was a cat, ready to pounce. She could hear the sound of the music coming from the saloon before the carriage even stopped outside of the building. And as the door was opened, she began to fear what was in store for her this night.

As Mr. Spark stepped down from the carriage, he turned around and offered Bethany his hand. She accepted it, more so because she liked having assistance down from the tall carriages. Yet, as she did so, she felt a sickening feeling enter her body as she felt how hot his hand was. It was a rather unpleasant feeling, but she was trying very hard not to be rude as she stepped down from the carriage. She withdrew her hand as soon as she was stable on the ground. Then, she slowly followed Mr. Spark into the noisy establishment.

Bethany noticed the delight on Mr. Spark's face as he pushed open the double swinging doors for them to enter. She was overwhelmed by the loud music coming from the band, the cheering from the crowd, and the overall tone of the voices in the building. Bethany stayed close to Mr. Spark only because she was nervous to be there and didn't like the looks she received from all the other men present. Considering that saloon girls were the only women to ever step foot in such a place, she was worried that the other men would think she was a loose woman.

"You find us a table and I'll get us a bite to eat," Mr. Spark said loudly over his shoulder to her. Bethany didn't like the idea of being alone in such a place, but she did as she was told and found the only empty table towards the back of the saloon. She didn't like how it looked and thought the wooden table and chairs were rather grimy. But she sat down nonetheless and waited for Mr. Spark to return.

"Hey there, good looking," said a man with a southern drawl. He approached Bethany and leaned down towards her. "Why don't we ditch the old man and go back to my place?"

"Please leave me alone," Bethany replied, hoping this creep of a man would just turn around and walk the other way. But her words only caused him to narrow his eyes at her as he leaned closer.

"I don't think that's how you're supposed to talk to a paying client," he said.

"I'm not a saloon girl," she said, leaning back from him. This seemed to catch him off guard as he then straightened up and really took a look at Bethany. He shrugged and walked away, finally leaving her alone.

Bethany wanted to bolt from the saloon and take off running down the streets if that meant returning to the safety of her home. She hadn't wanted to come to this place, and now she felt more trapped than ever in her life.

"Here we go, my dear," Mr. Spark said happily as he came to the table and set down two plates of food. Bethany looked down at her plate to see two pieces of oily fried chicken and a large helping of collard greens. "Best food in town, in my opinion."

Bethany gave him a small smile before she started to use her fingers to pick apart the chicken so she could at least eat something. But when her gloves began to become quite ruined from the grease, she gave up the pursuit and decided she would sneak off to the kitchen when she returned home. Now that she understood the basic principles of cooking, she could make herself something better to eat than what had been presented to her.

"Enjoying yourself?" asked Mr. Spark with a bright smile. His eyes were shifting about the room as he ate mouthfuls of fried chicken. He was absolutely revolting, and she wondered how she could get out of this situation. The saloon smelled of old beer and smoking tobacco, the combination making her body protest against even being in such a place.

"It's a unique experience," Bethany muttered, her eyes meeting those of other gentlemen that were taking in her appearance. She didn't like the way they were looking at her as though she had no clothes on at all.

"I like to bring my lady companions here and show off to the others that I'm able to dine with beautiful women when they are left to enjoy the thrills of loose women," Mr. Spark explained. Bethany focused her eyes on the man as she deconstructed what he had just said to her. It was so startling and revolting that she dearly wished she had come in her father's carriage so she could leave immediately. Instead, she decided she would do her best to disturb Mr. Spark as much as he had her.

"So, you're saying that I'm not the only woman you are currently pursuing," Bethany said as she pushed her plate away from her. Mr. Spark seemed to notice that she had given up on eating and didn't seem to appreciate that.

"You're the only one that I'm considering marrying, if that is what you're concerned about," Mr. Spark said in a frank voice. His eyes returned to the band, and she could hear how he was tapping his foot along to the music.

"I suppose I would be more concerned about the number of women you plan to be with after we are married," Bethany said. Mr. Spark chuckled as though she had just stated a joke.

"Come now, darling. Men in my position don't just sleep with one woman. I'm sure your father has a whole group of concubines he enjoys from time to time," Mr. Spark said, snickering as he did so.

"If my father does, he has never brought any such woman into our home."

"Of course not. That is why places like this exist. I'd even bet that most of these men are married. They're just looking for a good time with a woman that is not their wife. It's more thrilling that way," Mr. Spark explained. It only made Bethany feel dirtier than she already felt sitting in such a place. The music was starting to fray her nerves, and she stood suddenly with the intent of finding some way home.

"Do you want to dance?" Mr. Spark asked as he looked up at Bethany with wide eyes.

"No, Mr. Spark. I want to go home. I've had enough of this place and still think that this is no place for a proper woman," Bethany stated. "I'll walk home if I have to."

"If you walk out those doors alone, I assure you that one of these men will follow you and take advantage of you. Likely by force," Mr. Spark said, his eyes returning to the band. "Your best bet is to sit down and enjoy yourself."

Bethany seriously thought about her choices. She could sit down and obey Mr. Spark and use him as protection. She might be forced to dance with him, and whatever else he had planned for the night. Or she could walk out those doors and pray she found some way to get home safely. She knew that Mr. Spark would only return her back home after enduring a grueling night with him. So, what was she going to do?

"Mr. Spark, I demand that you take me home at once. This

is absolutely barbaric. Why do you think I'd agree to marry you after a horrific night like this?" Bethany asked, raising her voice a bit. She was starting to gather a small crowd of onlookers, and she could tell that Mr. Spark didn't like that by the way he set down his chicken suddenly and began to wipe his fingers and mouth.

"I am sure that your father will make you marry me either way," Mr. Spark said as he looked up at Bethany as she continued to stand there. "Your father has already promised me your hand in marriage. I would like to think you'd enjoy your time with me in a place that is forbidden to your upbringing. Surely there is a wild temptress underneath that modest clothing, one that would like the opportunity to be unleashed in a place like this."

"Mr. Spark, I'm sorry if I gave you any impression that I could be such a woman, but I am not. I'm a respectful human being that would very much like to leave such a sinful place," Bethany said. Those who were watching the conversation began to laugh at what Bethany had said, but she didn't care one bit. Perhaps the bigger the scandal she caused the more likely Mr. Spark would be to take her home. But when he started to eat the food she had discarded she began to feel as though she was losing any hope of going home right away.

"Is there a problem here?" asked a man that came walking up to the table. She noticed that there was a sheriff's badge pinned to his vest. It glistened in the lamplight and Bethany thought she could jump for joy at seeing a lawman.

"No, Sheriff. Nothing to concern yourself with," Mr. Spark said as he pulled out a ten-dollar bill and set it on the table. He then slid it in the direction of the lawman and Bethany watched, waiting to see what the sheriff would do.

"I need a ride home," Bethany said. "I don't want to be here anymore." The sheriff then looked at Bethany for a hard moment before looking back at Mr. Spark.

"Sounds like you need to use that ten dollars to hire this young lady a cab. This isn't a place for her kind," the sheriff said.

"I'm enjoying the entertainment and my company, Sheriff," Mr. Spark spat. "Sounds like you need to mind your own business before someone gets hurt."

The sheriff rolled his eyes as he took the ten-dollar bill and then motioned for Bethany to follow him. Bethany didn't hesitate, and she started to follow the sheriff back through the saloon towards the open door. Mr. Spark seemed to catch on to what was happening and started to holler after them. The sheriff spoke to two gentlemen at the front door and they both turned and faced Mr. Spark as the man tried to come after them.

Outside, the sheriff stepped into the road and hailed the first hackney that was passing by. When the cart came to a stop, he gave the driver the ten-dollar bill and gave the man specific instructions to take Bethany straight home and not to stop if he didn't need to. The sheriff then turned back to Bethany and offered her a small smile.

"I hope to never see you back in my saloon again, you hear?" he said.

"I promise you, Sheriff, that I will never come back here of my own free will. I assure you that I didn't have a choice in the matter," Bethany explained.

"I don't try to understand the actions of the rich, but I wish the best of luck to you, miss," the sheriff said as he tipped his hat towards her and then made his way back inside.

Bethany thought she heard Mr. Spark yelling after her, but she didn't wait around to know for sure. She pulled herself up into the cart and gave the driver specific instructions on how to get to her house. He then flicked the reins and sent his horse into a fast trot. As the Watering Hole faded away, she finally began to feel better.

Bethany wasn't sure what would happen when she returned home, or when her father found out what had happened. She would be ready to explain herself when the time came, and to express how dreadful the place was. There was no reason a woman like her should ever step into a place like that, and it took getting a lawman involved to save her from such a place. She knew that if she told the sheriff her whole story that he wouldn't be able to do anything for her. She belonged to her father, and when she married, that control would transfer to her husband. Women had no rights but to marry and give birth to children.

Silently praying that her father wouldn't notice her return, she thanked the driver as he pulled the cart to a stop in front of her house. She was already thinking of what she would say as she went inside, finally settling on something she thought was pretty clever. So, when she walked inside the house that evening and her father quickly came out of the study, she already had tears in her eyes.

"Bethany, why are you home so early?" he demanded to know.

"Oh, Father. It was absolutely horrible. There was a fight

and the whole saloon went crazy. Mr. Spark did his best to protect me. A sheriff paid for my hackney home," Bethany said with tear-filled eyes. Her father seemed flabbergasted and it took him several minutes to speak again.

"You should go get ready for bed. It sounds like you've had a horrible night," he muttered.

"The worst night of my life," she stuttered, fake tears falling from her eyes. She looked at the ground as she walked to her room in the servant's quarters, thankful her father didn't try to question her any further. She knew that eventually the truth would be told to her father and he would plan some sort of different punishment for her. But for the time being she was able to get ready for bed and get some sleep before the chaos of her life continued.

After changing out of her clothes and bathing as best she could in the water basin, she pulled on a nightgown and got into bed. She gathered the covers around her like a shield, wishing she could fall asleep and wake up somewhere very far away from her home. She thought about Tanner and what he might be doing at that moment. She knew that Bear Creek was being threatened by a group of outlaws and that things for him must be far worse than what she was experiencing in that moment. But she thought that despite all of it, she would rather be with him than in her own home.

As Bethany did her best to keep positive thoughts in her mind, like the fact she was no longer in the saloon and had been saved by that sheriff, she imagined what her life might be like with Tanner. She wondered if he was as kind as his letters made him out to be, and if he was handsome, unlike many of the businessmen her father had introduced her to in the past.

She thought about what their wedding day would look like and how nice it would be to actually have real friends. She appreciated Matilda's company, but wished to have friends she could rely on and help in return.

Though she tried to fill her head with pleasant thoughts, Bethany couldn't stop remembering what Mr. Spark had said about her father already promising her hand to him. She didn't think that her father could really force her to marry anyone. After all, she was the one that had to say 'I do' at the altar before the priest and everyone present. No one could force her to do that. She knew deep down inside that no matter what, she wouldn't marry Mr. Spark. She had seen firsthand that he was a pig of a man and not someone she could ever respect, no matter how much money he had.

CHAPTER 11

Tanner was so lost in thought that he hadn't even heard the sheriff come into the office. It took Jacob sitting down on the edge of Tanner's desk and waving a hand in front of his face to get him to focus on reality and not what had troubled his mind so much. He couldn't help but chuckle as he shook his head.

"I've never seen you think so deeply before," Jacob said. "What's on your mind?"

"I've been thinking about Bethany this morning," Tanner admitted. He knew he could talk to Jacob about anything and not have to worry about him blabbing like Mr. Fry would have. "I know how anxious she is to come out here because of her living situation. But I've been wondering if I should write to her and explain how coming to Bear Creek might not be the best idea right now. Or even Montana in general."

"Yeah, I would reckon the same thing," Jacob admitted.

"She could come out as far as North Dakota, but I doubt you'd like her staying by herself in a new place."

"I feel there's no right answer," Tanner said as he ran his fingers through his hair. "She has an overbearing father who will more than likely force her to marry a man she doesn't love. Yet, she might get into serious trouble if she comes out here. There's no clear choice."

"There isn't an easy choice," Jacob stated. "She can either marry a man she doesn't love and find a different type of trouble in life. Or she can risk coming out here and maybe running into trouble and no doubt falling head over heel in love with you." Tanner chuckled, thinking his boss was really putting on the humor today.

"Well, when you put it like that, it seems the best thing for Bethany is for her to come out here," Tanner said as he stood from his desk and stretched. He should be out patrolling instead of running his brain indoors.

"And it's the best thing for you as well, Tanner. It would be good to see your goofy face in love and married," Jacob quipped as he got up from the desk and went over to his own. He pulled out a telegram and set it on the makeshift map. Tanner watched as the sheriff made a few notes on the map about a town that was far east of them. It gave Tanner a feeling of hope that the outlaws wouldn't bother with Bear Creek. Perhaps they heard of the Sioux Indians and would stay clear of them. Then Tanner wouldn't have to worry about anything.

After bidding Jacob farewell, he went outside and untethered his horse at the hitching post. He then mounted the gelding and steered the horse out of town. If the latest news was that the outlaws were now to the east of them, then he would ride around the east side of Bear Creek and keep his eyes open for any signs of danger. But as he rode, the image of Bethany's portrait continued to rise in his mind.

He pictured them walking together through Bear Creek, just talking and getting to know one another. Tanner would be happy to show her how to ride a horse so she could get around easier, or perhaps how to drive a wagon. He could imagine them laughing together as Bethany found her balance on the horse and learned to steer it this way and that. He would be proud to help Bethany learn something new, and she would smile brightly at the whole experience.

There was so much that Tanner wanted to experience with Bethany. He wanted to fall in love with a woman for the first time in his life. He wanted to marry for love and have children he would enjoy raising with Bethany. He would no doubt continue to face dangers in life as a deputy, but he would always assure Bethany that he would be coming home, even if he lost a body part. Tanner snickered as he remembered the time Jacob broke his leg being thrown from a horse when it was spooked by a bear. There was no telling what could happen in Bear Creek.

Tanner was pulled from his thoughts as he saw a trio of Sioux Indians riding towards him. He stopped his horse and waited for the Indians to approach. Tanner knew that this was his opportunity to show that he wasn't afraid, that he could handle himself properly when speaking with these peaceful Indians. But the closer they got, the more afraid he became.

"Afternoon, Tanner Williams," greeted one of the Sioux Indians. "We wanted to see if you were in need of any assistance."

Tanner forced a smile to his face though his hands were clenched on the reins. “Thank you. I’m riding along the east side here because we’ve received word that the outlaws are now in a town far east of us,” Tanner explained.

“Then we shall go and tell our brothers of the news,” said another Indian as he nodded his head. Tanner nodded in return and finally took a long, deep breath as the Indians turned their ponies around and headed off in the other direction. Tanner sighed deeply as he encouraged his horse to continue on with the patrol. He tried hard to focus on the horizon and everything in the distance. Yet, his pounding heart kept distracting him.

BETHANY AWOKE to the sound of someone pounding on her door. It frightened her, and she instantly rolled over in the bed and pressed herself up against the wall of the room. Pulling the covers up over her head, she prayed the lock on the door would hold against the frantic pounding.

“Bethany! Get your rear end out here!” yelled her father. “I know what you did last night and you’re going to pay for embarrassing me!”

The last thing she was going to do was allow her father anywhere near her while he was so angry. He continued to rant and rave, to pound on the door with his fists. She heard some of the other servants trying to calm him down and convince him to have a drink of brandy in his study.

Her father’s raging continued. Bethany figured an hour went by before he eventually stopped and left.

Bethany was too scared to move from her spot on the bed. Her body was shaking, and tears were filling her eyes. She had no idea what she should do, but she knew that she couldn't stay locked in the room forever. She would need to eat something, and she was terribly hungry at the moment from not eating a good dinner last night and never having taken the time to make something for herself when she got home.

Bethany was sobbing into her bent knees when a soft knocking could be heard at the door. At first, the sound startled her as she thought that perhaps her father had returned to try to manipulate her into opening the door for him. But when she heard Matilda's soft voice, she quickly dried her eyes and strained to hear what her friend was saying.

"Let me in," Matilda said again, only this time Bethany could hear her better as she got off the bed and neared the door. Bethany was terribly nervous to do so, but eventually she unlocked the door and opened it. Matilda was standing on the other side with a tea tray and hurried in with it. Bethany closed and locked the door behind her just in case her father was stalking her room, waiting for an opportunity to strike.

"The whole household is in an uproar," Matilda said softly as she set the silver tray on the nightstand next to the bed. "Mr. Spark paid a visit this morning and Mr. Duncan is furious over hearing what happened last night."

"What was said?" Bethany asked, curious to know what story had been relayed to her father.

"Mr. Spark said that you drank yourself into a tizzy and danced with every man in the saloon but him. And that when he tried to take you home, you fought with him to the point that the sheriff had to get you a ride home," Matilda explained.

Bethany was so shocked that she placed her hand over her mouth as her jaw dropped open.

"That is preposterous," Bethany said. "I had become so uncomfortable in such a horrific place that even the sheriff noticed my distress and came to my aid."

"I believe you, Bethany. But it seems your father does not. He has been saying some awful things all morning."

"Oh, Matilda. I don't know what to do," Bethany said as she sat back down on the edge of her bed.

"You need to think about getting away from this place," Matilda said, coming to sit on the edge of the bed with her. "We've talked about it before and I think now is the time for you to gather a few things and leave Tennessee at once."

"I'm just so afraid that he will find me if I try to run," Bethany admitted.

"Yet there is a good chance that he will never find you if you run far enough," Matilda pointed out. "You could be gone on the next train out of town and never be found again."

Bethany wasn't so sure she could actually succeed. It was one thing to pretend she was someone she wasn't by disguising herself for long enough to make it to Bear Creek. It was another thing to hope that her father would ever give up on trying to find her. After all, his business stood to make a hefty profit when she married Mr. Spark, and she was sure her father would not give up on her that easily.

"Come. Eat something. Then I shall help you dress for the day," Matilda said, breaking through Bethany's thoughts. She eventually agreed, eating bits of toast and porridge that had peaches and honey in it. After she was done eating, she started to feel a little bit better. By the time she was dressed in a simple day gown made of cotton, she figured she'd at least try to help the other maids with the chores for the day.

Bethany got over her fear of her father, thinking there was nothing more he could really do to her besides beat her to death, and she knew that none of the servants would allow that to happen.

She went to the kitchen and helped Cook prep for dinner, and then she went outside to the garden to help tend to it with the other servants. Later in the afternoon, when she was coming in for a bit to eat while the freshly washed laundry hung on the line, she was approached by her father as he crossed the main room.

When she noticed her father coming towards her, Bethany stopped walking and turned to face him. Matilda was just down the hallway from her, and she knew her friend would wait for her, just out of sight. What startled Bethany most about her father's appearance was that he no longer looked mad. Instead, a grim smile was on his face. He stopped in front of her and folded his hands behind his back as though he was about to lecture her again.

"After the scandal of last night, Mr. Spark and I have come to a conclusion. The only way to save your reputation from complete ruin is for the two of you to marry in the morning," Mr. Duncan said.

"Father, Mr. Spark is a liar. If you would instead speak to the sheriff that owns the Watering Hole, he would give you the actual story and you would discover what really happened," Bethany said as she folded her arms over her chest.

"You can try to talk your way out of this all you like, but the priest has already been notified and the documents have been drawn up. In the morning you shall marry Mr. Spark and I'll be officially done with you," Mr. Duncan said. "The seamstress is on her way with a handful of premade gowns. You will choose one of them and she will fit it to you. Then you shall go to bed early after a light dinner to prepare for the wedding."

"You can't make me marry him!" Bethany shouted as Mr. Duncan turned and started to walk away from her. He stopped after Bethany had shouted at him, and as he turned around once more, Bethany became very afraid. He had a gleaming smile on his face, as though Bethany had just given him permission to seek whatever revenge he wanted on her.

"That's the best part, my dear. You don't have a choice in anything. You are just a woman who must adhere to the will of her father and husband. It doesn't matter what you say during the ceremony tomorrow. You will be married to Mr. Spark, and that is the end of it," he hissed with delight.

This time, when her father turned and left, Bethany didn't say anything. She was too shocked and dumbfounded to speak up and couldn't think of anything to say that would honestly matter anymore.

"Come on," Matilda said softly as she took Bethany's hand and led her to the kitchen. There, she made a relaxing tea for Bethany to sip on while Cook made some cucumber sandwiches. Bethany ate slowly, feeling as though her life was coming to an end.

Matilda stayed by her side when the seamstress came to the house with her three assistants. They entered the drawing room with several gowns for Bethany to choose from. She told the seamstress that she would be fine with any gown that would fit her. After trying on about six different gowns, a simple white one was chosen. The gown was made out of silk with short sleeves and a layer of lace that was stitched into the waist and flowed down to the hem. The train of the gown was not very long, and as Bethany looked at herself in the mirror, she thought it was a lovely wedding dress. She only wished she could wear it while marrying someone she actually loved.

Once the gown fitting was over and her wedding dress was ready for the next day, Matilda took the gown and brought it up to Bethany's old bedchamber. Bethany had been permitted to retire there for the rest of the day. Matilda even brought her a light dinner to enjoy as she sat down at her writing desk, trying to write a message to Tanner that would explain everything. Why she wouldn't be coming to Bear Creek to meet him. Why she wished she'd rather die than marry Mr. Spark.

Her father didn't come to say any words to her that night. Eventually Bethany ate some food and was about to get ready for bed when Matilda came to her room dressed in a dark burgundy gown. Servants in the Duncan household had to wear either black or brown, so Bethany was surprised to see Matilda dressed as though she was going to visit with some friends. She had a small smile on her face as she closed and locked the door behind her.

"Your father has gone to bed, having drunk enough brandy to require him to be carried to his bed," Matilda explained. "I had Benedict really focus on filling his cup tonight. He owed me a favor."

"I suppose I should get some sleep as well," Bethany muttered, her letter to Tanner crumpled in her hands. There was no way she would be able to post it to him anyway.

"No, my dear. We are going to get you ready to leave this place. And I'm coming with you," she said with a happy smile. Bethany stared at her friend for a moment, thinking that perhaps she had misunderstood the maid.

"What? You can't be serious," Bethany said in a whisper, afraid her drunken father might be able to hear them on the completely opposite side of the house.

"I'm very serious," Matilda said as she went to Bethany's bed and pulled out the traveling trunk from underneath it. She set it on top of the bed and opened it before going to Bethany's wardrobe and pulling out her traveling gown. Bethany hadn't been on many trips, so the gown had been left unused for some time.

"How are we going to escape this place?" Bethany whispered as she joined Matilda.

"There is a train heading west, leaving the depot at a quarter past eleven. We have an hour to get your trunk packed, and then we'll slip out the servant's door once everyone is asleep. I've already paid a hackney to take us to the train depot. He'll meet us down the road a bit," Matilda explained in a soft voice.

"You've already thought of everything," Bethany said softly. As she watched Matilda fold her simple gowns, the ones she used for housework, she started to become a bit excited. Her friend was not only going to help her escape, but Matilda was willing to run away with her.

"Hurry now and get dressed into your traveling gown and boots. I will pick the clothes that are most suitable for when we are living in the West. No need for fancy gowns, but practical clothing for housework," Matilda explained.

Bethany hurried and got changed, tossing her other clothes aside, for she no longer cared about them. She made sure to pack all the letters she had received from Tanner so her father wouldn't be able to discover where she had run off to. She also packed a handful of her most prized possessions, from the small bottle of perfume that had been her mothers, to her nice hair combs and hand mirror that had also been her mothers.

Once Bethany's trunk was packed, Matilda left her room to finish overseeing her own packing and to make sure there was nothing left in Bethany's other room in the servant's quarters. She would wait for Matilda to return, and then they would leave together. But as Bethany sat on her bed, biting her nails as nerves started to build up in her stomach, she thought of something she knew would really help them in their travels. Money.

Getting up from her bed, Bethany slowly walked to the door and pressed her ear upon it. When she was certain there was no one in the hallway, she opened the door and stepped into the darkness of the house. Very little light from the windows illuminated the house. As she slowly made her way to the stairs and down them, she was careful not to knock into anything and alert the footmen to her presence.

For the first time in her recent life, Bethany made her way into her father's study. She was grateful that the doors were still open so that she could easily slip into the dark room and make her way around the large mahogany desk to where she knew her father's safe was. Using her hands to feel around for it, she eventually found the handle and pulled it open. As she reached into the dark abyss, she felt several cloth sacks underneath her fingertips. She had no idea how much money was in each sack, but she gathered as many of them as she could carry.

Closing the hatch on the safe once more, the click piercing the silence of the house, she stayed knelt behind the desk for several minutes until she was certain no one had heard her. Then, carrying the heavy sacks upstairs, she made her way to her bedchamber and was able to breathe a sigh of relief as she closed the door behind her. Matilda had returned to her room and looked very worried. When she saw what Bethany was carrying, her eyes grew large.

"Oh no. Stealing from your father will only make matters worse," she whispered as Bethany loaded the items into her trunk. She opened one of the sacks and removed a few bills that she then stuffed into her pocket. She shut the trunk and started to clasp all the locks on it.

"Running away is going to make him madder than a hive full of bees being knocked to the ground," Bethany said. "And this will ensure that we can travel easily enough." Matilda didn't protest as she picked her own trunk off her bed. Bethany opened the door for her as she stepped outside first. Then, even though it was very heavy, Bethany picked up her own trunk and followed closely behind.

Bethany's heart was hammering in her chest as she followed Matilda through the dark house. They had to go slowly so as not to trip or make any sound, so they didn't make any hasty moves. Once they got out of the house, it would be far easier. They took their time and walked down the hallway, down the servant's stairs, and then out the servant's door that opened up into the back gardens.

The fresh air felt amazing against Bethany's skin as they

hurried around the lawn and towards the main road. She could hardly believe she was running away from her home after the countless times she had thought about it. And the fact that she was doing so with Matilda was like a dream come true. Now she knew she wouldn't need to go alone and that she would have her closest friend with her. As the only person who knew that she'd been writing a deputy in Montana, it was a good thing that Matilda was coming with her so she wouldn't have to face the wrath of her father.

As promised, a hackney waited for them down the road. The driver jumped down and helped the women with their trunks, Bethany's arms becoming weak as she was relieved of the heavy burden. She didn't wait to pull herself up into the cart and turned around to help Matilda do the same. They even held hands as the driver got back up into the driver's seat and flicked the reins to send his horse moving at a fast pace.

"We did it," Bethany said happily, leaning towards Matilda so only she could hear her.

"Only once the train has left the depot with us on it will I actually feel as though we have succeeded," Matilda said honestly. Bethany nodded, knowing her friend spoke the truth.

When they reached the train depot at fifteen minutes to eleven at night, they thanked the driver as he helped them with their trunks. Matilda went to the ticket box to arrange their passage, and Bethany paid the driver a large bill. He was surprised as he looked down at it.

"If anyone asks, you never saw us and you most certainly did not give us a ride to the train depot," Bethany said softly to the man.

"Your secret is safe with me," he said as he dipped his

head. He hurried back to his hackney and turned the cart around. Bethany watched as he flicked the reins hard and urged his horse to race away from the train depot as though he was being chased.

"Here are our tickets," Matilda said as she came back to Bethany's side. She looked down at the ticket through the lamplight and saw she had secured them an entire compartment to themselves. She was now glad she had risked so much to steal from her father. The money would surely allow them to travel in comfort.

"I also gave the ticketer fake names," Matilda explained as they walked together towards the train. "If anyone asks, your name is Megan Davenport while we are traveling, and I am Susan Smith."

"Sounds good to me, Susan," Bethany said with a chuckle. Together they showed the train attendants their tickets and had their trunks taken to their compartment. They followed after the attendants and were shown to the large compartment. Their trunks were stored overhead on racks and they were shown how the seats could be folded out to form a decent-sized bed. The ladies thanked the attendants before they left, and Bethany tipped them well on their way out. When the sliding door to the compartment was closed, Bethany locked it before turning back to Matilda.

"This is so exciting," Bethany said as they sat down on the padded seat together. They turned their gaze to the window and watched as others quickly boarded the train as the whistle was given that the train would soon be departing.

"I never thought I would be leaving this town," Matilda said. "But I am happy to go with you, Bethany. I don't have any family here, and I couldn't bear the thought of you either marrying or leaving by yourself. I'm sure the West will have plenty more opportunities for us, and we could stick together through it all."

Bethany wrapped her arms around Matilda and hugged her tightly. She was doing her best not to break down into tears. She was so happy that her friend had done so much for her. Matilda hugged her back, chuckling a little as she did so.

"Everything is going to be alright now," Matilda said right before the final whistle blew for passengers. "By this time tomorrow we shall be far away from Tennessee, no matter how many trains we have to take to reach Montana." Bethany just nodded her head, feeling so much relief at once that it overcome her. For a long time Matilda just held Bethany as she completely fell apart.

CHAPTER 12

Tanner was certainly used to Mr. Fry barging into the sheriff's office with an important telegram for Jacob, so when Mr. Fry came running to the office, Tanner thought nothing of it. He was rereading a few of Bethany's letters before he went out on patrol. But when Mr. Fry handed the telegram to him instead of Jacob, his eyebrows furrowed with concern.

"The message just came over the line," Mr. Fry said as Tanner looked down at the message. He noticed that the origin was Kansas City, Missouri, and his first thought was that he didn't know anyone in Missouri. But as he read the message, all came clear.

"Bethany and her friend are on a train headed for Bear Creek," Tanner said as he stood and walked across the way towards Jacob. He handed over the telegram while Mr. Fry just looked between them.

"Who is Bethany?" Mr. Fry asked.

"Official business, Mr. Fry," Tanner said with a kind smile. "Can't be sharing that kind of information."

"Of course," Mr. Fry said as he dipped his head. "You fellows have a good day." Tanner thanked the shopkeeper for delivering the message before he left the building. And then he turned worried eyes on Jacob.

"Not the best time to be coming to Bear Creek," Jacob said with a sigh, handing the message back. "Everyone is on high alert. More families have moved into town. I don't even know if the stagecoach will keep coming this way if the driver fears danger."

"At least she's not alone," Tanner said as he reread the message. "Something must have happened to convince her to leave now."

"I'm sure we can both assume what happened, Tanner. I just wish there was a safer place for them to stay until this trouble can either blow over or be dealt with," Jacob said as he stood from his desk and put on his Stetson. "Best be off doing patrols."

"Sure," Tanner said as he pocketed the message and headed outside with the sheriff. They both mounted up and began their patrol of the town, followed by a wider sweep of the east side of the area. The entire time, Tanner thought about Bethany and how she must be doing traveling so far for the first time. He hoped that she was trying to enjoy the experience and didn't find it too terrible. From what he'd heard from the other women in town who had made the journey, like Mrs. Benning from Boston, Massachusetts, it was about a two-week trip that could be rather uncomfortable.

Yet, despite all the danger Bear Creek was facing, he felt

excited at the thought that before too long he would get to meet Bethany in person. He dearly hoped that they could grow close and marry, and he'd finally be able to have the family he had longed for since his parents died of sudden diseases.

The fact that Bethany was traveling with a friend meant that there would be another single woman in Bear Creek, and that would no doubt make some of the men very happy. Even though they were experiencing tough times, he couldn't deny how happy it made him to think that Bethany was on her way, she was doing alright, and she wasn't traveling alone.

"Get your head out of the clouds, Tanner," Jacob called over to him as they rode out through town. Tanner focused on the task at hand then, nodding to his boss as his eyes started to scan the horizon instead of just staring off into the space in front of him. But as a smile grew on his face, he couldn't help but feel so happy in that moment, despite the dangers they faced.

It took until the Tennessee border for Bethany to feel as though she had successfully escaped her father. She and Matilda had switched two trains before reaching Missouri. And once they had reached the large town of Kansas City, Bethany figured it would be a good idea to telegram Tanner and give him a heads up that she and Matilda would be arriving. She made sure to use no names so if her father was watching the telegram lines, he wouldn't be able to tell it was her.

For the most part, Bethany was finding traveling by train

to be both exciting and enjoyable. She liked seeing the country pass by the window, and sometimes she would just stare outside for most of the day, waiting to see what else she could see. Other times she and Matilda would talk about their future. Matilda was showing her how to do some simple needlework so she could keep her hands busy while they traveled.

Bethany would say that nighttime was the hardest part of traveling. She and Matilda had a comfortable enough bed when they folded up the bottom parts of the benches. It was just the constant rocking and clacking of the train going down the metal tracks that would often wake her suddenly at night. She had nightmares about her father and Mr. Spark coming after her and doing horrible things to her. She often took small naps during the day, feeling more comfortable when Matilda was able to keep an eye out for her.

Eating was an interesting challenge on the train, as was seeing to their basic needs and maintaining decent hygiene. Though there was a dining car, Bethany and Matilda found they could get better food at the train depots. The train only stopped for an hour at each stop, so they had to be quick about getting a bit to eat or stopping in one of the bathhouses to use a water basin to freshen up. The bathhouses were for men mostly, so there weren't many options for women.

But the further west they traveled the less resources were available. Soon there were no restaurants and instead tiny cafes attached to each train depot to get a bite to eat. Bethany and Matilda started having to rely on the simple food that was served in the dining car. The food grew to be of less and less decent quality, and then cost more to purchase by the time they reached North Dakota. But Bethany knew not to complain, because she had a pretty good idea of what she would be experiencing if she was still in Tennessee, now married to Mr. Spark. He might have had all the money in the world, but she still would have been completely miserable.

"Did Tanner ever write about possible employment opportunities?" Matilda asked one day. They were soon reaching the part in their trip where they would have to start taking a stagecoach down through Montana to reach Bear Creek. Bethany was looking forward to sleeping in a real bed and having a nice long bath to wash away the grime that had collected on her skin. She understood that life was harder in the west because there was less convenience, and less access to certain resources. But she could only reason that women had found how to do things differently in remote towns to obtain the same result.

"No, I hadn't asked about employment," Bethany said honestly. "With what Montana is currently experiencing, I'm sure there won't be too much hiring going on."

Matilda sighed then as she looked out the window. "I wonder how I'm going to be able to care for myself if I don't find employment right away," she said. Bethany chuckled as she took her hand.

"My dear, you have nothing to worry about. I will make sure to take care of you, for I have enough money for the both of us to live off of for some time. I hope to marry Tanner if we find each other suitable. And I'm sure you'll meet a man that you'll come to love. Then we shall both be married women and have nothing to worry about," Bethany said cheerfully.

Matilda smiled at her, but Bethany could tell that it didn't quite reach her eyes. "I just don't want you to think that you *have* to take care of me," Matilda said.

"Come now, don't think in such a way. I owe you my life, Matilda. And I am going to repay you one way or another. It is your courage that started us off on this journey, and it will be the one that sees us through it all," Bethany said with her chin raised high. She watched Matilda's smile turn into an honest one then and felt very proud of what she was able to do for her friend. Bethany wasn't sure just how much money she had stolen from her father, but she knew for certain that it was a lot.

When Bethany and Matilda were rather bored, they would take turns sitting in the public cart with the majority of the passengers. One would remain behind to keep an eye on their trunks. They couldn't be too careful when Bethany had so much money in her trunk. They would take turns walking up and down the train for exercise or sitting in the public car to converse with different passengers.

"I hear there has been lots of trouble in Montana," said an older woman to her traveling companion. Bethany assumed that they were husband and wife. And at the mention of Montana, she made her way towards the woman and sat down on the bench in front of her, exchanging pleasant smiles.

"I couldn't help but overhear that you're speaking about Montana. Is that where you are going?" Bethany asked.

"California," the woman explained. "My younger sister is there, and I wish to be with her."

"Your sister must be very excited to see you," Bethany said. The older woman smiled happily while the older man looked grumpy and put off.

"I can't wait to reach California. I shall see the ocean for the first time in my life, and my sister has promised to take me to all the nicest shops," the older woman enthused.

"That sounds quite lovely. My sister and I are traveling to Montana," Bethany explained.

"Oh no, not Montana," the woman said, her expression quickly changing to one of dread. "I've heard about these outlaws that are giving the settlers a lot of trouble there. And for no good reason, as far as anyone can reckon. That's all I heard on the train yesterday."

"We'll be reaching Montana in a few days, and then taking the stagecoach a bit further south," Bethany explained. "I hope we won't run into any trouble."

"I hope for you as well," the woman said. "Pray tell, what is your name, child?"

"My name is Megan Davenport," Bethany said, having become used to the foreign name after having introduced herself many times. "Massachusetts." She had been choosing different states each time so she would become harder and harder to remember.

"Nice to meet you, Miss Davenport. This is my brother, Charles," the woman said. "And I am Daniella."

"It's a pleasure to meet you both," Bethany said, but as she shifted her eyes to the brother, he simply harrumphed and looked out the window.

For a bit longer Bethany sat with the older woman and listened to her talk and talk about California and her life back in Ohio. It was nice to listen to another person's story; you just never knew what you might hear on the train. And it seemed that Daniella hadn't had many people to talk to, so she freely spoke to Bethany while she just listened in return.

Around supper time, Bethany excused herself and went back to the compartment that she and Matilda were sharing. She found her friend happily doing her needlepoint, humming a soft tune to herself. Bethany settled onto the bench across from her friend and turned her gaze to the passing scenery. The horizon was beginning to stretch further and further away from the train as they entered prairie lands.

"It sure is gorgeous out here," Bethany said as she took it all in. "I can see now why people move so far away to live in a place like this."

"It's certainly a change from a bustling town in Tennessee," Matilda agreed. "I hope we will both enjoy being all the way out here."

"I know we will," Bethany said confidently. "It may be different, and we might be forced to seriously adjust, but I think we will both be a lot happier than we had been back home." Bethany didn't even want to talk about Tennessee anymore, so she avoided the word at all cost.

After taking turns going to the dining cart, they began to get ready for bed. Tomorrow the train would stop in Great Falls, Montana, and from there they would travel by stage-coach for many days to reach Bear Creek. And even though this next leg of the trip would no doubt be very uncomfortable as they rode in a stagecoach for endless hours, it did not make Bethany grumble one bit. She was happy to have escaped her father and looked forward to being settled in Bear Creek in a few short days.

CHAPTER 13

Tanner had taken up the habit of being at the general store every time the stagecoach was expected to be in town. He had no idea when Bethany would be arriving with her friend. But he wanted to be there just in case she did show up. Each day after lunch time, Tanner would make his way to Fry's to stand outside on the porch and wait for the stagecoach until about four o'clock. Then he would patrol with Jacob until it was too dark to see.

Things had become tenser in Bear Creek after Jacob received a telegram saying that the outlaws had moved to another town a little further up. Details of their chaos had been included in the message from the marshal, and Tanner was surprised by the devastation. Entire small towns had been burned to the ground, forcing people to flee or die fighting. It all confused Tanner to no end, because he couldn't understand what would influence a group of men to do such a thing. And why hadn't anyone been able to fight back successfully?

Tanner had started to hear all sorts of stories around town of what people were thinking about doing. Some thought they could hightail it south while the outlaws were moving north. Then they would start their lives over and not have to worry about trouble hanging over their heads. But Tanner reasoned that the outlaws would return the way they had come once they grew tired of what they were doing. He figured no place was safer than home, especially if the outlaws decided to leave them alone all together.

Jacob had mentioned to him that he was thinking about having Mrs. Benning and their daughter go stay with the Sioux up at camp. It would be much harder to attack an entire tribe up in the mountains. The Indian scouts would spot anyone sneaking through the woods before they were able to make it to camp and cause any trouble. Therefore, he reasoned, it was the safest place around.

"Perhaps the best plan for retreat would be to go up into the mountains," Tanner had suggested.

"That's a good idea, Tanner. I'll talk to Brown Bear about it. If everyone who's able to fight evacuated the town when the outlaws came looking for trouble, then at least we could save as many lives as possible if they end up out numbering us," Jacob had decided. Tanner felt better knowing that a back-up plan could be put into action if all the Sioux warriors, plus those in town who could fire a gun, weren't able to take out the outlaws and put a stop to their rampage.

Tanner was pulled from his thoughts and musings when he noticed the stagecoach was coming into town from the north. A large plume of road dust rose up behind the stagecoach as it rattled down the dirt road at a fast pace. The driver and shotgun rider both had to keep a schedule, as many people depended on them for resources and supplies. At the sound of the stagecoach reaching the town, Mr. Fry came out on the porch to greet the driver and help with any packages that were for him.

"Let's make it quick, Mr. Fry," the driver said as he came to a stop, set the brake, and hopped down from the bench with speed. "We're headed south and not planning on making any more runs 'til Montana is a safe place again."

"What have you heard?" Tanner asked, not even noticing the stagecoach door had opened from the inside.

"It's what we've seen, Deputy," the driver said as he and his shotgun man got to quick work unloading the back of the stagecoach. There were a bunch of crates for Mr. Fry, and that's when Tanner noticed two trunks as well. "Last stop was a total ghost town. Nothing but remnants of burnt buildings. We didn't even stop."

Tanner could hardly believe the news. But the bigger shock came when two young ladies stepped down from the stagecoach and looked around. Tanner instantly recognized Bethany from her photo and stepped forward to great her.

"Welcome to Bear Creek, Miss Duncan," Tanner said with a bright smile. He was brimming with excitement at finally getting to meet her. "I'm Tanner Williams."

She smiled up at him. "Mr. Williams. It's a pleasure to meet you at last. This is my dear friend, Matilda Rayford," Bethany said, gesturing to the plump woman beside her who had long brown hair and matching brown eyes. Tanner greeted her as well, noticing how tired and worn out they looked.

"The inn is just down the road," Tanner said. "I can escort

you both there so you can get settled. The Tibets own the establishment and have a room set aside for single, traveling women."

"Sounds wonderful," Bethany said as she went to pick up her trunk. But Tanner was quick to intervene.

"You can leave those here with Mr. Fry. He'll make sure no one runs off with them. I'll see you two to the inn and I'll come right back for them," Tanner promised. Bethany didn't look convinced, but eventually took the arm that Tanner offered her. He gestured his free arm towards Matilda, and she smiled as she took it.

"A true gentleman," she said as they began the walk to the inn. Bear Creek wasn't a very large town, and he took the time to point out different places to the women.

"There is a clinic, a barbershop, a bank. The way you came through town is where the sheriff's office is, the boarding house for most of the miners, and a butcher. There is a shop on the south part of town that caters to the miners since that is Bear Creek's main source of revenue," Tanner explained.

"Would you highly recommend the bank?" Bethany asked. "I have a large deposit to make."

"Yes, Mr. Fritz and his wife are both honest, hardworking people. I trust Mr. Fritz with all my money because he has a shotgun behind the counter he isn't afraid to use if trouble comes to the bank. Even with all the talk of the outlaws in Montana, I haven't touched my money and leave it safe with Mr. Fritz," Tanner explained.

"That is good to hear," Bethany said, sounding relieved.

"Mr. Williams, are you familiar with any employment

opportunities?" Matilda asked. "I have many years of experience working for the Duncan household, and though I don't expect there to be well-off families in Bear Creek, I'm hoping to use my skills for other job opportunities."

"I'll have to think on that one, Miss Rayford. Everyone is more concerned about the outlaws than anything else at the moment. But I am sure we can think of a creative solution," Tanner said, trying to remain hopeful. It was easier for him to think about the number of single men in Bear Creek than the jobs that were currently available for a single woman.

Once at the inn, Tanner lowered his arms and introduced the women to Mr. Tibet, who was often standing at the front desk. Tanner saw how the dining room was mostly cleared out of the normal tables and was now full of cots. He noticed how a few of those cots were actually occupied, and it made Tanner worried about the level of fear in town.

"Ladies, if you don't mind sharing a room, I have a special room just for mail-order brides at the bottom of the stairs down this hallway," Mr. Tibet explained as he pointed towards the room. "Mrs. Tibet and I reserve it for such women because we want them to feel safe in a new place. Our suite is right across the way, so you can always come get us if you need anything. We're even willing to share our water closet." Tanner noticed the happy expression on Bethany's face at the mention of the modern amenity.

"That's very kind of you, Mr. Tibet," Bethany said. "And Matilda and I don't mind sharing a room. We've been sharing a train compartment for the last two weeks and haven't grown angry at each other yet." The young ladies chuckled together, and Tanner could see that they had a close bond. He was curious about the pair of them since Bethany had never mentioned a Matilda before in her letters.

"Well, let me show you to your room," Mr. Tibet said as he picked up a key that had been hanging on the back wall behind the counter.

"And I'll be right back with the trunks," Tanner assured as he left the inn and made quick work of the chore.

"Those are some mighty pretty ladies there," Mr. Fry commented as he came back to the store for the trunks.

"Sure are, Mr. Fry. But don't you let Mrs. Fry hear that," Tanner said, causing the old man to chuckle.

"Are both of them here to court you?" Mr. Fry retorted.

"I'm not that lucky of a man, Mr. Fry. But one of them is, yes. You let all the single men know, that a new single lady has just come to town. The brown-haired one," Tanner said, figuring Mr. Fry was the best person to tell information to because he was quick to let others know.

"You bet," Mr. Fry replied as he worked on taking all the supplies inside.

It took Tanner two trips to get both trunks to the ladies' room. They were both heavy, and Tanner could only assume that the women had been traveling with everything they owned, which wasn't much at all since the trunks were small. He was glad to see that both of them found the room to be suitable for their needs.

"If you like, I'll come back around dinner time and we can get to know each other," Tanner suggested as he addressed Bethany.

"Dinner sounds lovely," Bethany replied.

"I think I will take dinner in bed," Matilda spoke up. "It's been such a long time since I've seen a proper bed that I don't believe you'll be able to convince me to leave it ever again."

"Understandable," Tanner agreed, his lips quirking in a grin. "Well, I'll see you later." He smiled at Bethany, hardly believing that she had finally arrived. He was anxious to hear her story and to spend time with her, but he knew that she needed to rest just as much as her companion. So, he dipped his head towards her and left the inn, thinking he'd best get the patrol over with so he could spend dinner with Bethany.

Tanner was all smiles as he headed over to the sheriff's office. There, he saw Jacob mounting his horse and preparing to go out on patrol again. Tanner was quick to join him, anxious to tell his closest friend the good news.

"What's got your face twisted up in a smile like that?" Jacob asked the moment he gave Tanner a good look.

"Bethany and her friend just arrived on the stagecoach," Tanner explained. "I got them both settled at the inn."

"Hot damn, it's about time," Jacob said happily. "No wonder you're all smiles."

"I'm glad they made it to Bear Creek without issue. The stagecoach driver said he won't be back through town until the danger is all over with," Tanner explained as they trotted out of town, heading north this time.

"That isn't great news," Jacob said. "Bear Creek will be hurting for fresh resources if the stagecoach isn't coming through right now."

"Makes me think that these outlaws better hurry up and come to Bear Creek so we can wipe them all out," Tanner reasoned.

"Don't take these men lightly, Tanner. They've managed to

destroy several towns and overcome a lot of able men who no doubt died trying to protect their lands and families. We might have an entire Indian tribe on our side, but there's no telling what these men are capable of," Jacob said.

"You're right," Tanner said with a sigh. "I just hope this will all be over with soon."

"Me too," Jacob said with a grin. "Because before too long there is going to be a wedding."

"You mean when Brown Bear and Sandy Roberts finally tie the knot?" Tanner quipped.

"Oh, you know what I mean," Jacob said with a chuckle. They settled into a comfortable silence then as they kept a lookout for any large groups heading their way. Tanner was so excited that Bethany was in Bear Creek he could hardly contain his excitement. But knowing how important it was to keep an eye open for trouble, he focused on the horizon, hoping he never saw any sign of the outlaws.

CHAPTER 14

Bethany was beyond relieved to finally be in Bear Creek and settled in a decent room at the inn with Matilda. Both women made quick work of drawing their own baths and enjoying the hot water. It felt heavenly after weeks of only having access to a little bit of cold water to keep themselves relatively clean. They took turns washing each other's hair, and Bethany was really starting to feel as though Matilda was more her sister than just a friend who used to work for her father. As they curled up on the bed after getting cleaned up, Bethany fell right to sleep next to Matilda, thankful for a real bed and pillow to sleep with.

When the sun was starting to set, Bethany woke up from her nap. She felt a bit sore from all the traveling they had been doing, but she was excited to have dinner with Tanner that night. She had been looking forward to spending some quality time with him for two weeks and now would finally have the opportunity to do so. Not knowing how much time she had left until Tanner would come looking for her, Bethany hurriedly got dressed in a nice blue gown and did her best at braiding her long blonde hair.

"You look lovely," Matilda said in a sleepy voice from where she lay on one side of the bed.

"Thank you," Bethany said with a bright smile. "I hope Tanner will think so as well."

"That man is already in love with you," Matilda said with a chuckle. "I saw how happy he was to see you, and knew from the beginning that he would be perfect for you. He is a real gentleman, and that's the type of man you need in your life after all you've been through."

"I really hope Tanner turns out to be one of the good ones," Bethany agreed. "I could really use a good man for the first time in my life." Her voice became soft as she spoke. She didn't want to think about the past any longer and thought that it would take some time still to forget it all.

"I'll bring you back something to eat," Bethany said, pushing the thoughts out of her mind.

"I'd appreciate it," Matilda said as she closed her eyes once more. Bethany dabbed on some of the perfume she'd brought with her before stepping out of their modest room. She could hear all sorts of chatter as she shut the door behind her and locked it with the room key. Bethany then walked down the hallway towards the commotion to see that the dining room was filled with people. Some were having dinner, while others sat on cots, minding their own business. It was a strange sight to see, and it reminded her of the reality of what was happening in Bear Creek.

"Have a good rest?" came Mr. Tibet's voice. She looked to see him standing behind the reception counter.

"Yes, sir. Both Matilda and I were able to rest up nice," Bethany said. "We sure appreciate your hospitality."

"Such kind manners," Mr. Tibet said with a bright smile. "I just wish you two didn't need to deal with all this fear we've been feeling here in Bear Creek. Most of us aren't sure what we're going to do if outlaws do come and try to raise trouble."

"I'm sure the sheriff and Deputy Tanner are working hard to keep the townspeople safe," Bethany reasoned.

"Yes, they sure are doing a great job. They even got the Sioux Indians working for them. But after the number of towns these outlaws have destroyed, a lot of us wonder if it will be enough," Mr. Tibet said honestly. Bethany nodded, understanding why people would be afraid. It was as though everyone had a reason to be afraid as she looked around once more. She was terrified of her father finding her one day. And these people were afraid about their basic need to live freely and without having to worry about someone coming to take that all away from them.

Bethany's mood brightened when she saw Tanner come walking through the door. She was quick to greet him, looking forward to the dinner they would be having together.

"How are you doing, Miss Duncan?" he asked.

"Please, just call me Bethany," she replied. "And I am doing fine. Matilda and I are both settled and well."

"I'm glad to hear that, Bethany," Tanner said softly. She felt a chill of excitement pass over her at the sound of her name on his tongue. She sure liked it a lot. "I have something special set up for you outside since it's a little crowded in the dining room tonight."

"Oh, alright," Bethany said as she followed Tanner outside. She saw that a small table and chairs had been set up a little bit from the inn with two candles resting on top to shed plenty of light. Bethany thought that was rather romantic and was excited to sit down at the table with Tanner.

"This is beautiful," she said as she looked at the checkered tablecloth. It wasn't fancy like what her father would have on his dining table. But knowing that Tanner had taken the time to put this all together meant more to her than what money could buy.

"I'm sure glad you like it," Tanner said with a soft smile. "I'm going to head inside and get us something to drink. Figure I'd give Mr. Tibet a hand."

"Sure," Bethany said with a nod. She watched him make his way back inside the inn while Bethany took a moment to look around the town. With the setting sun, there wasn't a whole lot she could see in the fading light. But she was overcome with a sense of relief. She'd made it to Bear Creek without any sign from her father. It made her wonder if she would really be able to live the rest of her life without ever having to see the man again. If that were true, she'd live a very happy life even with the threat of outlaws.

It didn't take long for Tanner to return carrying two wooden cups full of water and Mr. Tibet right behind him with two plates of food. "Hope you don't mind spaghetti, Miss Duncan," Mr. Tibet said. "Mrs. Tibet and Mrs. Benning have to cook only one type of dish a night since resources are going to be low for a while. But I promise you it's the best spaghetti you've ever had."

"I know for certain I'm going to love it because it is way better than any food Matilda and I have had since we started traveling," Bethany said. "I'll be sure to bring her a plate of food later as well."

"Certainly," Mr. Tibet said before he returned inside.

"I'll admit, I wasn't expecting spaghetti this far west," Bethany said as Tanner settled into the seat across from her.

"Mrs. Benning has taught Mrs. Tibet quite a few recipes since she moved here. She grew up in Boston, Massachusetts. You just never know what those two are going to cook up. Sometimes it is comfort food like biscuits and gravy, or pork chops. And then it gets real fancy when they make pasta or meat pies. Mrs. Tibet's shepherd's pie is famous in town."

"Eating a home-cooked meal is like taking a bite of heaven," Bethany said as she picked up her simple fork and started to turn a forkful of pasta on it. She then took a large bite, something her father would say was rather unladylike. However, she wasn't trying to be a perfect lady anymore. She was simply trying to enjoy a good meal with a man she hoped to marry one day soon.

Bethany moaned softly at the delicious taste of fresh pasta and tomato sauce. Little bits of meat had been mixed into the sauce, and before she knew it, she was digging right in. She hoped that Tanner didn't particularly mind her large appetite. After having less than good food to eat for two weeks, she thought the spaghetti really was the best she had ever eaten.

"My word. I don't think I've ever seen a woman eat like

that," Tanner said once she had finished. Bethany blushed as she wiped her mouth on her napkin. She felt suddenly shy then and wondered if she should have restrained herself a little more.

"I feel as though I haven't eaten a decent meal in a long time," Bethany explained. "I promise I don't always eat so hurriedly."

"I'm not saying it's a bad thing," Tanner reassured. She noticed the way he started to blush as well and thought perhaps he felt embarrassed now. "It was just an observation, I assure you." Bethany smiled, hoping to put him at ease and show him that she wasn't offended.

"If I get the opportunity, I'd like to cook for you sometime. Cook helped me learn a few dishes I wouldn't mind recreating. I'm not sure if I'll be able to get my hand on the ingredients, so maybe I'll have to get creative," Bethany said.

"I look forward to it either way," Tanner replied. "I'm sure the last few weeks have been pretty hard on you." The mention of her past caused Bethany to still. She was certain that Tanner was curious as to why she and Matilda had suddenly left Tennessee, and she gathered up her courage in order to tell the whole story.

"For me, it was pretty hard," Bethany said. "I'm sure there are many in my situation who would have gone along with whatever my father proposed because it meant being wealthy. But I couldn't agree to marry a man I didn't love, no matter how much money he had. And I had started to learn that Mr. Spark was truly the worst of men. And my father no better.

"It was Matilda who had the courage to help me run away.

The fact that she was willing to go with me was even better. She was a maid in my father's house, and we had become close friends when my father decided to have me work as punishment. I couldn't leave her there with the knowledge of where I would be going. So, when she said I had to leave the day my father announced I would marry Mr. Spark the next morning whether I wanted to or not, I gladly went along with her plan.

"She helped me pack, and I admit that I stole quite a bit of money from my father. I used it to pay our way here." Tanner was kind enough to let her speak and didn't interrupt her once. She wasn't used to a man actually listening to her, but then wondered what his response would be.

"I don't blame you for coming out here," Tanner said. "And I was so glad to hear that you were not traveling alone when I got your telegram. But I wonder what your father might try to do to find you. How much money did you take from him?"

"I haven't counted it all," Bethany admitted. "But it is probably enough that I could live comfortably for the rest of my life." She watched as Tanner's eyes grew large. He would be even more surprised if he learned that what she had taken was only what she could carry, and that there were many cloth sacks still in her father's safe in his study.

"I'm sure your father isn't very pleased with you, both for running away and stealing from him," Tanner said. "Yet, I still don't blame you for what you did. It is wrong of him to force you to marry someone you don't want to be married to, or who you won't at least agree to marry on your own." Bethany nodded, liking how Tanner wasn't mad at her. Her father had seemed to be mad with her all her life, and now that she was starting to like a man, she never wanted him to be mad at her for anything. She was done with all the yelling and screaming in her life, done with wondering if her father was going to start beating her.

"I hope I never see the man again," Bethany said in a soft voice. Tanner reached across the table then and took her hands in his. She'd never held a man's hands before and blushed again.

"Even if he comes to Bear Creek, I won't let anything happen to you," he said. "Once all this blows over here in town, I think we should start planning our wedding."

"You... you already like me enough?" Bethany asked shyly. Tanner smiled kindly at her as he nodded.

"You haven't given me a reason not to," Tanner said, squeezing her hands lightly. "I can tell that you're a pretty brave woman, leaving a bad home like you did. I know your friend must have made it easier, but you were the one who made the decision to leave when you were offered the opportunity. You're the type of woman I can be proud about, and once you get settled here in town, I'm sure you'll really start to like it here, too."

"I already love it here," Bethany said with a bright smile. "It's simple and small, but I love the wide-open spaces so much. There are no bustling roads, or people trying to prove themselves to one another. It's just the perfect little town."

Tanner laughed as he let go of her hands. She missed the feeling and hoped to find reason to hold his hand again in the future. "You sure have a real good opinion of Bear Creek when you've only been in town for a few hours," he said.

"After everything I've been through, I can really appreciate a place like this," Bethany explained. "I'm looking forward to meeting the people here and helping Matilda get settled. She's done so much for me that I know it would only be proper for me to do all in my power to help her as well."

"We'll do it together," Tanner reassured. "I believe there is plenty of opportunity in Bear Creek for those who are able to see it and take advantage of it. There are other single men in town Matilda might find interesting as well."

"I sure like the sound of that, doing things together," Bethany said with a sigh. "I've always wanted to work together on something, not just be told what to do or how to do it, or even worse, told to just sit down and look pretty."

Tanner chuckled as he nodded. "I can't imagine what you've been through, Bethany. But I'm sure glad you're here now."

Bethany's heart was brimming with joy as their dinner ended. Tanner was nice enough to offer to clean up so she could head to the kitchen and pick up a plate for Matilda to enjoy as well. But as she went to the counter to inquire, Mr. Tibet happily explained that he'd already gone to the trouble. After thanking him kindly, Bethany made her way to their shared room, happier than she probably had been in her entire life.

Bethany was about to talk to Matilda all night long about her wonderful dinner, but she realized that her friend had not only eaten but had fallen back to sleep. After taking care of the dishes by taking them to the kitchen, Bethany returned to her room to change back into her nightgown and get some sleep herself. It was hard for Bethany to fall asleep that night because she was so excited to finally be in Bear Creek and know that one day soon she'd be married to a man as fine as Tanner Williams.

CHAPTER 15

Tanner could hardly contain his smile as he made his way towards the sheriff's office the next morning. He'd risen early and taken care of all his animals while he whistled a happy tune. Then, once he was freshly shaved and in a clean change of clothes, he rode into town to check in with Jacob. Tanner hadn't realized he hadn't stopped whistling until he was stepping into the sheriff's office and Jacob had raised an eyebrow at him.

"Morning there, lover boy," Jacob said with a chuckle. Tanner placed his hands on his hips and just narrowed his eyes at his friend.

"Not nice to call people names," Tanner retorted as he walked up to the desk and looked down at the map. It didn't seem like anything had changed from the day before, and Tanner hoped that meant that Bear Creek was in the clear.

"So, is she everything you dreamed of?" Jacob asked, trying hard to contain his mirth. He'd never seen Tanner so happy in his life and thought they could all use a bit of humor during this tense time.

"Bethany is quite amazing," Tanner said as he went over to his desk and perched himself on the edge. "She's kind and funny. Has a great positive attitude. And she explained why she and her friend came so suddenly. She was in a real bad place, being forced to marry a man she wanted nothing to do with. It was her friend, Matilda, who actually gave her the courage to go."

"Well, I can't fault a woman for running away from a bad situation like that," Jacob reasoned.

"I would absolutely agree with you. However, she also stole a hefty amount from her father's safe before she fled town with her friend. That's the part I'm worried about," Tanner admitted.

Jacob sighed deeply as he ran his fingers through his hair. "If her father ever finds out where she is, we might have a situation on our hands," Jacob said. "And we already have a big enough situation to deal with that we don't need any more trouble in Bear Creek."

"Well, if he ends up coming out this way any time soon, perhaps the outlaws will just take care of him and then that will be that," Tanner said with a shrug of his shoulders.

"Life doesn't always work out so easily," Jacob said as he pointed a finger at Tanner. "The both of us will need to be on the lookout and listening for Bethany's father to be headed this way as well. If he had the power to force a woman into marriage, God only knows what the man is capable of. Especially a wealthy man who's just had his money stolen."

"Then I hope he never figures out where she went," Tanner

said with a sigh. He had just turned around to sit down at his desk and double check that his pistol was clean and ready to go when there was a knocking on the door. Jacob got up and answered it, opening the door all the way to let three Indian scouts step inside.

"Good morning, Jacob Benning," one said in a grim voice. Tanner quickly put away his pistol and stood. The Indians glanced at Tanner for only a moment before focusing their eyes on the sheriff. "We have come to deliver the grave news. The outlaws have been spotted north of the area, heading south along the main roads."

Fear gripped Tanner's heart instantly. The dreadful news everyone had been praying would never be spoken had now been delivered. Tanner ran his hands through his hair, feeling a bit shaky. He took several deep breaths to calm himself so he could assist Jacob the best he could. Now was the time for action.

"How far are they from town?" Jacob asked.

"Three day's travel. The Sioux are keeping a close eye on them from a distance. Other riders have gone to warn Brown Bear that soon all able men and woman will be needed to defend the people," the Indian explained.

"Thank you," Jacob was quick to say. "I must go now to tell the mayor, and to prepare everyone."

"Very good," the Indian said, followed by a grunt that Tanner learned was a sign of approval. He then motioned for his fellow Indians to follow him as they left the office. Tanner felt he could breathe a little bit easier as he took several deep breaths and prepared to take swift action.

"Alright, Tanner. Let's get moving. First, we tell the

mayor, and then we start warning the rest. Time to get the people safely in town and set up blockades on the northern road," Jacob said as he pulled on his Stetson. Tanner was right there with him, ready to follow orders to keep everyone safe. Yet, as he stepped outside the sheriff's office with Jacob as they went straight to the town hall, his eyes drifted towards the inn where he knew Bethany and Matilda were. He'd been so happy to finally meet Bethany and to see she truly was a woman he could marry. But now that danger was coming to town, he prayed that he'd be able to keep her, and everyone else, safe from the outlaws.

THERE WAS a bright smile on Bethany's face when she woke the next morning. She could hear Matilda humming softly as she got ready for the day. Bethany rolled on her back and stretched, thinking how nice it was to get so much sleep in an actual bed for once. Matilda must have been watching Bethany, as she chuckled when she saw what Bethany was doing.

"I still can't fully believe we made it," Bethany said with a smile. "And I had such a wonderful dinner with Tanner last night. It fully confirms that this was the best choice, coming all the way out here."

"I'm glad you feel that way," Matilda replied. "I find this small town very quaint and can't wait to see more of it today. I'm ready to get to work and find my place here in Bear Creek."

"Don't be in too big of a rush," Bethany said as she got out of bed and started to pull back the covers so it was nice and tidy. Matilda joined her as they finished up the chore together. "I did promise to take care of you. And when I have this money deposited in the bank, we shall be fit for the rest of our lives."

"But you will no doubt be marrying soon," Matilda pointed out as she helped Bethany choose a gown to wear that day. They would need to do their laundry so they could have fresh clothes to wear once more. "Your money will then go to your new family."

"Matilda, listen to me. It doesn't matter when I marry. I will always take care of you," Bethany said as she stopped what she was doing and placed her hands on Matilda's broad shoulders. "If it weren't for you, I wouldn't be here right now. I would be married to a horrible man and completely miserable."

"You give me too much credit," Matilda said in a shy voice.

"That's because you deserve all the credit. You were the one who gave me the opportunity to change my future. I shall never forget that," Bethany said before she changed for the day in her most suitable gown. It was nothing fancy like she would have worn back home. It was simply a dark brown dress that would be suitable for cleaning laundry.

A knock on the door pulled them from their conversation. Matilda, being more ready for the day, answered the door while Bethany was still trying to braid her hair so it would be up and out of the way. A woman's voice came from the door, and Bethany turned from the small looking glass to see an older woman.

"I'm Mrs. Tibet," she explained. "I wanted to come and check on you two to see how you are doing this morning." Matilda opened the door further and let her enter before shutting the door once more.

"Mrs. Tibet, it's a pleasure to meet you. I did thoroughly love the dinner you prepared last night," Bethany said.

"Thank you, dearie," she replied, yet her smile didn't quite reach her eyes. "Mrs. Benning and I will soon be fixing up breakfast. You two are more than welcome to join us, as there is plenty. However, I wanted to come and share some bad news." Bethany stopped fussing with her hair and gave the woman her full attention.

"I'm sure you've heard about the outlaws already," she said. Both Bethany and Matilda nodded in reply. "Well, the sheriff is spreading the news now. They've been spotted heading our way, coming from the north. They'll reach us in three days' time."

Fear raced over Bethany as though she was a lightning rod and she'd just been struck. She shivered, trying to get the feeling to go away. She had known about the outlaws for weeks from Tanner's letters. But to know that all of Tanner's worries were coming true made her afraid to think what Bear Creek would do next. And more so, what she should do to prepare. No one had been able to stop these outlaws yet and she wondered if this would be the end of her life when she felt it was just getting started.

"I know it's a big shock, but Bear Creek has faced a lot of dangers before. Mr. Tibet and I have observed some of the worst weather a person could experience, and even unusual sicknesses. I have a lot of faith in the sheriff and the people of

Bear Creek. And even the Sioux Indians, who will help to protect us," Mrs. Tibet said in a confident voice. Bethany wished she could feel as confident as the woman sounded and instead just nodded in understanding.

Mrs. Tibet left the room then, and Matilda and Bethany were left to look at one another. They had no skills in fighting, and they both wondered silently what they should do. Eventually, Matilda helped Bethany finish her hair before the two of them left the room to get something to eat. They wouldn't be able to do anything on an empty stomach, and figured eating would be the first step for today, no matter what the day brought.

CHAPTER 16

Tanner was surprised at how quickly everything happened. By the afternoon, all the shops and businesses had been temporarily closed so every able person was available to either ride out of town and bring family in, or help build a handful of barricades that would be taken north on wagons to be set up along the road. When a low drumming had filled the air, Tanner had stopped hammering nails into boards for a barricade to watch as Brown Bear appeared on the back of an Indian pony, his chest painted as though he was ready for war.

Deep down, Tanner knew that having the Sioux on their side was important for the town and the surrounding areas. But seeing them ready for a fight made Tanner's stomach tighten with dread. The last thing Tanner wanted to see was Indians fighting when he knew for certain it would bring back all sorts of horrible memories he really wanted to forget. Therefore, he gave his tools to another and quickly went over to the inn so he wouldn't have to watch the Sioux getting settled in town to help defend them all.

At the inn, he felt a little more relaxed. The dining room had been converted into a place for people to sleep and rest. The remainder of the tables had been moved out of the room and cots now filled the space from one wall to the next. Every hour it seemed another family came into town. Between the inn, the boarding house, and the town hall, they would no doubt be able to house all the farming and ranching families. Seeing that everything was running smoothly, he walked down the hallway and knocked on Bethany's door, hoping to see how she was doing.

"The girls are out back," Mr. Tibet called down the hallway as he stepped out of the kitchen. "Doing laundry."

"Thank you, Mr. Tibet," Tanner said as the man continued into the dining room carrying extra linens to disperse.

Tanner made his way through the kitchen, saying a quick hello to Mrs. Tibet and Mrs. Benning before stepping out of the back door of the inn. Behind the building was a large chicken coop, and a little way around the side was the well where he found Bethany and Matilda. But as he observed the several wicker baskets of clothing, he wondered if this all belonged to the two women.

"Afternoon, ladies," he said with a smile as he approached. He saw how Bethany's face lit up as she saw him coming their way. He liked to see her smile. Especially after all the grim news they had received that day.

"Why hello there," Bethany said as she stood and dried her hands on her apron. She looked nothing like the debutante she'd described herself as in her letters. Tanner would have guessed she'd been raised on a farm, accustomed to the work needed to maintain one's home and family.

"I see you two have been busy," Tanner said, gesturing towards all the laundry. There was quite a bit already hanging on the clotheslines behind them, the garments and linens drying in the slight breeze.

"Well, we started washing our own laundry, and before we knew it all sorts of people were asking us to do theirs as well," Bethany explained.

"And the pay isn't bad, either," Matilda was quick to add. Tanner chuckled as he placed his hands on his hips, surprised by how quickly these two had thought of a great business venture.

"That's certainly a very nice thing you're willing to do for people," Tanner said. "With all sorts of people coming into town, even the simplest of things will be harder."

"Tanner, would you mind accompanying me to the bank? I have a large deposit to make and would like some assistance," Bethany said as she finished drying her hands. After all the washing they'd been doing, her hands looked a bit raw and in need of a break.

"Certainly," Tanner replied.

"You two take your time," Matilda said. "I got things covered here."

Tanner gave Matilda a nod before following Bethany back inside the inn. He waited for her to collect her things in her room as he stood by the front counter, taking it all in. Tanner watched the families in the dining room talking with one another and trying to entertain children. He watched their body language, seeing how tense their shoulders were. He hated to think that anything would cause such fear in people, but he reminded himself that they were doing all they could to keep the people safe, even if the outlaws made it to Bear Creek and there was a big shootout.

He was pulled from his thoughts when Bethany joined him once more, carrying a laundry sack on her back. It looked rather large and Tanner was quick to take the load from her. He was surprised by the weight, wondering how Bethany had managed it all on her own.

"Let's get going then," Tanner said with a smile on his face as he walked with Bethany. She held the door open for him as they left the inn and walked up the boardwalk towards the bank.

"I really appreciate you doing this for me," Bethany said. "I was a bit nervous just walking the short distance to the bank."

"I don't blame you. This is a good weight. You disguised it well," Tanner said as they passed a group of men looking like they were heading to the inn for something to eat. "Wouldn't want anyone to know what I was really carrying." Bethany chuckled, nodding as they went.

As they stepped into the bank, they found Mr. Fritz at the counter with his wife. They looked to be in a heated discussion, and Tanner felt bad for interrupting them.

"Why hello there, Deputy. Good to see you. And who is this fine young lady?" Mr. Fritz asked as his wife huffed and went around the partition wall. In the back, Tanner knew, was where Mr. Fritz kept his safe. As the only banker in Bear Creek, the next bank being a two day's ride south, Mr. Fritz did well for himself. This was the place all the miners brought their gold to exchange for real bills.

"Mr. Fritz, I would like you to meet Miss Bethany Duncan. She and her friend Matilda Rayford came in on the stagecoach yesterday. Miss Duncan has a deposit she would like to make," Tanner explained as he set down the laundry bag on the counter. Mr. Fritz eyed it, and as he opened and peered inside, his eyes grew large.

"That's quite a sum you have there, Miss Duncan. I would normally say welcome to Bear Creek with a big grin to know such economy has come to town. However, with our current situation, I can at least promise all of this will remain safe," Mr. Fritz said, a smile on his face.

"I appreciate it," Bethany said. "I'm sorry to have interrupted your previous conversation."

"Ah, you don't worry about my missus. We just had a difference of opinion, but nothing serious," Mr. Fritz said with a smile. "Well, Miss Duncan, this will take me some time to count. However, when I have finished and have it all put up in the safe, I'll write you a certificate and bring it to you myself."

"Thank you, Mr. Fritz. Miss Rayford and I are staying at the inn," Bethany explained.

"Then I shall see you this evening," Mr. Fritz replied. After saying their goodbyes, Tanner and Bethany stepped outside to see a number of different activities happening around them. It was truly a sight to see, and as they stood together watching it all, Tanner couldn't help but reach over and take Bethany's hand. She looked up at him then, her brow furrowing.

"I don't want to sound negative, but if these outlaws are

really going to cause all sorts of trouble for this town, I want to be able to hold your hand as much as I can now while I still have the opportunity," Tanner explained.

"I completely understand," Bethany replied, tightening her hold on his hand. Together, they walked hand in hand back around the inn to where Matilda was still washing the laundry. He thought the incoming pile had grown since they had left.

"Well, I have all sorts of work to get to myself, overseeing quite a few small projects. But I'll be sure to visit with you this evening," Tanner said as he let go of Bethany's hand.

"I look forward to it," Bethany said with a smile on her lips. Despite all of the chaos that seemed to be happening around them, Tanner felt like he could find relief and focus on Bethany, helping him to remain calm.

Tanner bid the two ladies a good afternoon as he made his way back around the inn. Wagons were streaming into town, carrying entire families and plenty of personal belongings. He hoped that these outlaws wouldn't try to vandalize any of the farms and ranches that were currently being temporarily abandoned. Only essential workers would be traveling out to the farms and ranches each day to do the bare minimum. Tanner certainly didn't want anyone getting caught off guard trying to maintain their livelihood.

By that time, the town was a mix of local settlers and the Sioux Indians. It made Tanner nervous as he walked towards the town hall where all the local officials seemed to be gathered. Brown Bear was there dressed in nothing but his buckskin leggings and a large bone necklace with many beads that signified his position as an Indian chief. His torso was painted in what looked like white chalk. Tanner wasn't sure what it all meant, but it was certainly intimidating to him.

"How are things going on your end?" Jacob asked Tanner as he approached the group.

"Barricades are being made. I stopped by the inn for a moment and saw that the finished barricades have already been hauled out of town," Tanner informed the group.

"They will do little but to let the outlaws know that we are ready for them," Jacob said.

"My warriors will continue to keep a close eye on their progress," Brown Bear said. "I think we should go out to meet them and conduct the battle in the open space away from town."

"I would like to avoid fighting at all costs," Jacob said as he placed his hands on his hips and sighed. "These outlaws have managed to destroy many towns, killing what might be in the hundreds. They are supposedly less than forty men. I don't understand how they are accomplishing this."

"If the reports are true, there are many Indians with them," Tanner stated. He then looked to Brown Bear and asked, "How would an Indian attack a town of people?" Brown Bear smiled as he thought about the question.

"An Indian's strength is stealth and surprise attacks. I would send a few to distract the main part of my enemy. Then, my warriors would attack from behind when they least expected it," Brown Bear explained.

"Then perhaps we are focusing our efforts in the wrong place," the mayor said. "Barricades should be made and placed along the south roads as well."

"The town is surrounded partially by the mountains and

forest," Tanner said, looking up towards the peak of the mountain that loomed overhead. "We will need to keep an eye out from that direction as well."

"Leave the mountains and forest to me," Brown Bear said with a confident smile as he crossed his arms over his chest. "I will not let intruders anywhere near my people."

"Well, it seems we have a plan, gentlemen. Let's get to it," Jacob said as he lowered his arms and headed straight for the men who had been working hard all day on the barricades. Tanner was certain those men wouldn't be pleased to learn that they had to make a dozen more structures. But whatever they could do today and tomorrow, the better the town would no doubt be.

"So, Tanner Williams, I hear that there is a new woman in town," Brown Bear said, a smile on his face as he approached the deputy. Tanner focused his attention on the Indian chief and did his best not to panic.

"Yes. Mail-order bride," Tanner said, keeping it short.

"I wish you much happiness. You deserve to be very happy," he said.

"Really? I do?" Tanner asked, thinking this was an unusual statement from an Indian he hadn't spent much time with.

"You serve this town diligently. The sheriff is very proud of you. You deserve to be happy with a wife and children," Brown Bear reasoned.

Tanner nodded as he said, "Thank you." He really wasn't sure what else to say, since this was the longest conversation he'd had with an Indian in a long time. Brown Bear grunted his approval and then walked off, talking Sioux with his fellow Indians.

Tanner could only imagine the Indians were working on some sort of plan to make sure the town wasn't left vulnerable. He took a moment to look all around him at the busyness of their small town. He felt proud to work alongside others to preserve what had been maintained for three generations now. Though he might be filled with nerves, he would never turn his back on these great people.

CHAPTER 17

By the time the sun was starting to set, Bethany was feeling exhausted. It was a good feeling knowing she'd put in a full day's work to help as many people as possible. Matilda was pleased with the work because it had earned them a small bit of money that Matilda felt very reassured about. Of course, Bethany told Matilda to keep all the money because that wasn't what she needed right now.

After folding all the dry laundry and returning it to the folks it belonged to, she and Matilda sat outside of the inn where the tables and chairs had all been set to allow people a place to eat as long as the weather continued to cooperate. She and Matilda were eating biscuits and gravy, something neither one of them had eaten before but both seemed to thoroughly enjoy. It was good, hardy food after a long day's work. And Bethany could eat it easily enough with her sore, pruney hands.

"Care if I join you?" said a voice. Bethany looked over to see Tanner standing there with a plate of food in his hands.

"Sure thing," Matilda said since Bethany had become tongue-tied. She found Tanner to be quite handsome, and even though they had exchanged several letters, she still felt a bit shy. This was the man she was going to marry, and every time she saw him, she couldn't help but feel excited about that idea.

"Seems like a busy place tonight," Tanner said as he sat down at their table and looked around. All the other tables were full.

"I heard there were some extra hands in the kitchen today to give Mrs. Tibet all the help she could want," Bethany said, finding her voice once more. "I suppose since many people are not in their homes like normal they are trying to maintain their lives by helping out elsewhere."

"Just like you two did with the laundry," Tanner said.

"I'm sure we'll be just as busy tomorrow," Matilda said happily. "I may have to open up my own laundry business after all of this is said and done."

"Wouldn't that be nice," Tanner said. "I'm sure all the miners will be coming to you, but I can only imagine how hard it would be to get their clothes clean."

"I'm not afraid of a little challenge," Matilda said happily. She then focused more on her food, giving Bethany and Tanner some time to talk with one another.

"Any news on what might be happening?" Bethany asked. She didn't want to talk about such dreadful things but figured it would be better to remain informed than simply wishing all of the danger would not come to Bear Creek.

"There are some theories floating around," Tanner

explained after he took a bite and chewed it properly before speaking. "These outlaws have been raising trouble all over Montana. We were thinking a lot today about why that might be, and why no one has been able to stop them. I'm nervous around Indians, but I'm sure glad the Sioux are willing to help us."

"Yes, I did happen to see some Indians today. I won't deny that I was frightened simply because I've never seen them before," Bethany said honestly. "But I will trust you if you say they are friendly and helpful."

"I have no doubt in that," Tanner was quick to reply. "Brown Bear, the chief of the Sioux, is the type of man you could just walk up to and talk with any day. He speaks good English and is always willing to listen to anyone. His people are very helpful, and I have no doubt his warriors will protect us."

"That is a relief to hear," Bethany said, a smile appearing on her face. "But even with all the Indians and the men in town, will it be enough to protect everyone?"

"I like to think so. We have far more men than what is being reported concerning the outlaws. I think what makes us even more dangerous than the outlaws is that we have to preserve our way of living. We're all invested in this place, in the town, and the farms and ranches in the distance. This is our home and we really don't have any other place to go."

Bethany was moved by Tanner's words. She was surprised to feel the same as he did. Bear Creek was the place she wanted to live now, far away from other big towns and cities. She wanted to raise a family in this place and learn to do things for herself. Bethany knew she would be a lot happier here than she was in her old life. Having all the money in the world and hiring people to do things for her was not her idea of happiness. Bear Creek was the type of place you could be proud to live in, and the people who called it their home as well seemed like fine neighbors.

When they were finished eating, Matilda was nice enough to offer to take their dishes back to the kitchen. Bethany thanked her kindly before turning her attention back to Tanner. He smiled at her, and his grin melted her through to her core. She couldn't believe how lucky she was to have met a guy like him, even when the town was being threatened by outlaws.

"Why don't I introduce you to some of my friends?" Tanner offered. "With so many families in town right now, it would be a great time to meet some new people."

"I would love that," Bethany said, thinking of the times she imagined meeting the people Tanner had written to her about. Matilda would always be her best friend, but the idea of making new friends who were used to living in Bear Creek gave her hope that she too would be able to adapt to the remote town.

"Bethany, may I introduce you to one of the oldest families in town, the Jenkins'," Tanner said as they wandered over to a larger table that was filled with a decent-sized family. "You have Mathew and Jenny, their children Mikey and Penelope. You met the Fritzs earlier. Mrs. Fritz is Jenny's mother."

"It's a pleasure to make your acquaintance," Bethany said as she curtsied.

"I recognize a debutante when I see one," Jenny said as she stood from the table and shook Bethany's hand. "I came from Virginia with my mother."

"Tennessee, with my lady's maid and best friend," Bethany replied in turn. "You have a lovely family."

"Thank you. I hope you'll feel welcome here in Bear Creek, despite all the dreadful news," Jenny said.

"I already love everything about this small town," Bethany happily said.

"Welcome to the area," Mathew Jenkins said with a nod. Jenny returned to her seat to help Penelope with her dinner while Tanner led Bethany further into the crowd.

"Dr. Roberts, may I introduce you to my bride-to-be, Miss Bethany Duncan," Tanner said as they approached a small table. Bethany blushed at the sound of being called a bride by Tanner, but thought it was not only appropriate, but very charming to hear out loud.

"Nice to meet you," Bethany said as the doctor quickly wiped his mouth on a handkerchief before standing and shaking her hand.

"Pleased to meet you, Bethany. This is my wife, Emily Roberts," Dr. Roberts introduced. The woman stood and shook Bethany's hand, and Bethany was surprised to see that the woman was wearing jeans. She also winked at Bethany, and it was obvious to her that she'd been caught staring.

"And this is my sister, Sandy. She is hard of hearing but reads lips pretty well," Dr. Roberts explained as the young lady with flaming red, curly hair stood and shook Bethany's hand. She was equally surprised by this woman's gown because it looked rather Indian. Sandy smiled happily at Bethany, and she just returned the gesture because she wasn't sure if words were necessary.

"Sandy will be getting married sometime this summer

when things settle down here in town," Dr. Roberts explained. "She is engaged to Brown Bear." Bethany had to think about the name for a moment, and then remembered that Brown Bear was the Indian chief.

"That is unique," Bethany said in a weak voice, so totally surprised that a white woman would be marrying an Indian chief. There were chuckles all around, and she felt rather embarrassed. She wasn't used to the concept and wasn't sure how to react.

"Don't worry, Bethany. We're not laughing at you," Tanner said as he took her hand, lacing his fingers with hers. She liked the warmth of his hand and instantly felt better. "Anyone would have the same reaction to learning who the Indian chief was marrying."

"I'm very excited to marry Brown Bear," Sandy signed to her brother, which he translated for Bethany to hear.

"Then I am happy for you," Bethany told her. It seemed to brighten her smile even more.

Tanner and Bethany bid them a goodnight as Tanner led her by the hand around to almost all the tables. She met miners, business owners, farmers, and ranchers. Bethany had never met so many new people in one night, having been raised in the same town all her life, interacting with the same wealthy families year after year. So, meeting so many people of different backgrounds with different reasons for being in Bear Creek really made Bethany even more excited to have come to such a wonderful place.

By the time Tanner had finished making all the introductions, Bethany's head was spinning happily. She was sure she wouldn't be able to remember all of their names, but she was happy to have met them. Tanner walked slowly with Bethany towards the inn, which had become quite a busy place as all sorts of families had come to stay in town. Even the clinic was serving as a temporary place to live, and all of the town seemed to be crowded even as night set in.

"Seems I should head home and get some sleep before tomorrow. It will surely be another busy day," Tanner said as he let go of her hand. Bethany already missed the warmth she had been enjoying and reasoned that they could start planning their marriage together as soon as the outlaws were dealt with.

"I know there must be a lot to do, but if we get a chance, I'd like to see you again tomorrow," Bethany said.

"You can count on it," Tanner said. Bethany noticed he was blushing, and then in the next moment he had leaned forward and kissed her on the lips. For a second, Bethany didn't realize what was happening. And by the time she closed her eyes to enjoy her first kiss, it had ended. She looked at Tanner and saw that his face was beet red. She couldn't help but smile brightly.

"Thank you," Bethany said. "I really enjoyed that after such a busy day."

"Me too," he said, letting out a deep breath he seemed to have been holding. "Well, I'll see you tomorrow, then." She waited by the inn door and watched him go, thinking she would be looking forward to tomorrow just to see him.

Bethany made her way into the inn, the sounds of hushed whispers filling the air as mothers tried to convince their children to relax and get some sleep. With such a big change in scenery, Bethany could only imagine how hard it would be for some people to get used to sleeping somewhere new. She had experienced the same thing when riding the train to Bear Creek. She would never again take for granted the feeling of a full-sized bed.

Bethany found Matilda resting in bed as she came into the room. Matilda was reading the novel Bethany had brought with her, but by the look of her drooping eyes, Bethany figured her friend would be falling asleep shortly. But Matilda set the book aside and focused her attention on Bethany as she came in and started to gather her nightgown to change into.

"How did your night with Tanner go?" Matilda asked before releasing a long yawn.

"It was lovely. He introduced me to practically the whole town," Bethany said with a chuckle. "I was sure able to meet a bunch of new people."

"That's good. As a deputy's wife, you should be familiar with the people in town."

"I still have a hard time wrapping my head around the fact that I'll be married soon," Bethany said as she got ready for bed. "I just arrived in a new town, and already I'm being introduced as a bride-to-be."

"Well, that is the reason you started writing Tanner. Right?" Matilda asked.

"I started to write him because I wanted to marry someone I could actually love. I'm not sure if I'm in love with him yet, but he is certainly the type of man I could love. I think more than anything I just wanted more control over my future," Bethany admitted.

"And now you certainly have that," Matilda reasoned as Bethany started to unbraid her hair. It came loose in ribbons of gold that she thought would look nice tomorrow simply tied back with a bit of ribbon.

"Matilda, are you worried about these outlaws?" Bethany asked, wondering how her friend was feeling through all of this.

"I suppose that it is a situation I shouldn't take lightly," Matilda said as she sat up a little. "From what people have been saying, these outlaws have already done a lot of damage to other small towns in Montana. And I think the scariest part is that no one seems to understand why they are doing it, nor has anyone been able to stop them."

"Yes, that's what has me concerned as well. I believe Tanner when he says that there are plenty of people here to help defend the town," Bethany said as she extinguished the lantern in the room. Matilda turned to the candle at her bedside table and snuffed it. Then, Bethany got into bed next to her friend and pulled the covers up over her.

"I've never really imagined being in a place with Indians," Matilda said as she got settled in bed. Bethany lay on her back, looking up at the ceiling with the help of the moonlight coming in from the windows.

"Yes, it is certainly a change from Tennessee," Bethany agreed. "I even met a young lady tonight who is white with beautiful red hair. She's going to be marrying Brown Bear, the leader of the Sioux."

"Really? Of her own free will?" Matilda asked, sounding surprised.

"Yes. She said that she was excited to marry him and was wearing Indian clothing as well. I've never seen such a thing in my life. It's like Bear Creek is the place where anything is possible as long as it's good for you and others," Bethany said.

"Then perhaps that means a woman like me can start my own laundering business?" Matilda asked.

"It would be easier, I'm sure, if you were married and ran the business with your husband. You know that women are frowned upon if they try to go into business on their own."

"Yes, I know that," Matilda said with a sigh. "But I can't help but want to do so, nonetheless."

"Well, I wish you all the success in the world," Bethany said as she found Matilda's hand and squeezed it for a moment before rolling over and shutting her eyes. Bethany knew that tomorrow would be a brand new day, filled with all sorts of opportunity and uncertainty.

CHAPTER 18

When Tanner rode into town the next day, he thought about the time he could be spending with Bethany. Perhaps he could give her a horse-riding lesson in the corral at the livery stables. There would no doubt be plenty of horses in the stables for Tanner to choose from that would be best suited for a woman who was riding a horse for the first time. But all of Tanner's positive thoughts for the day seemed to vanish as he rode into town and saw the grim look on people's faces as they stood outside the clinic.

"What's going on?" he asked Curtis Denver, the local butcher. He was a lumberjack of a man and could often see over a crowd. Tanner rode up beside him and didn't have to look too far down to address him.

"Peters and his two boys went back to their farm this morning to work the fields. They arrived to find their barn and house on fire. They tried to put out the flames themselves and got burned up pretty bad," Curtis explained. Tanner gasped at the news, looking towards the clinic with the rest of the crowd.

Tanner hurried off his horse and tethered the reins to the nearest hitching post before he started to address the crowd. "Alright folks, that's enough of that. Time to get moving along. I'm sure Dr. Roberts is doing the best he can."

"What's going on, Deputy?" a man called back at him. "Why wasn't there anyone to protect the Peters family?"

"Can't protect a man from his own choices, Mr. Miller. I probably would have done the same thing," Tanner admitted. "Now move on and mind your own. We'll get through all of this if we just stick together."

There were some mumblings, but eventually everyone stopped crowding around the clinic and moved on to do something else. Tanner had just convinced everyone to get moving when the sheriff came hurrying down the road towards him.

"What did I miss?" Jacob asked when he neared.

"Rode into town this morning to see a crowd outside the clinic. Seems the Peters returned to their farm to find it aflame. They tried to combat the flames themselves and only got hurt," Tanner explained. "That's all I know from Curtis Denver."

"The Peters' farm? But that's way out in the east," Jacob said, taking off his hat and slapping it against his thigh in frustration. Tanner nodded, feeling the same. They were told the outlaws were in the north, heading south. Now it seemed they were coming from the east. And, if Brown Bear was correct, they might try to sneak in from the south when they weren't expecting it.

"Let's head to the sheriff's office and wait for the morning report from the Sioux. They should be heading in any moment," Jacob suggested. Tanner nodded his agreement. He collected his horse and led it over to the sheriff's office. And just like Jacob thought, the Sioux came riding in just as Tanner finished the last slipknot on the reins to the hitching post.

"Sheriff, bad news," the first Sioux Indian said as he slid off his pony and quickly came forward. "Five burning teepees in the area. East and south."

"Do you mean homes and barns?" Jacob asked. The Indian wrinkled his nose for a second, thinking about the English words, before nodding his understanding.

"The living places of the whites, for them and their animals," he explained.

"What about the scouts that have been keeping an eye on the outlaws coming from the north?" Jacob asked.

"The outlaws had disappeared in the night. By morning, our scouts cannot find them. We think these people are Blackfoot. Very sneaky," the Indian explained. Jacob cursed under his breath while Tanner felt a wave of panic crawl across his skin. He'd heard about these types of Indians before and felt a great sense of uneasiness.

"Seems like we must prepare from all sides," Jacob said, giving Tanner a look. Tanner nodded, already trying to think of some quick plan of action. "My friend, please update Brown Bear. Spread word for all the scouts to come to town. We must prepare to defend the town and the people here."

"Very wise decision, Sheriff. We will go and spread the word," the Indian said before turning to his fellow warriors and speaking the instructions in Sioux. They all seemed to get the message as they turned their ponies around and raced out of town, quick to take action.

"I wonder who the other four families are?" Tanner asked out loud, feeling as though he was spinning from the reality of it all.

"It's too dangerous to ride out and see for sure," Jacob said, turning his attention on Tanner. "We need to spend the day preparing people, keeping everyone in town, and preparing to face these mongrels."

Tanner only nodded, knowing that words would not be enough to convey their feelings of deep anger. This was families' entire livelihoods that these outlaws were messing with. And with that feeling of anger, the two got straight to work. Word of what had happened spread like wildfire, causing everyone to react pretty much the same way. They were angry, but Tanner and Jacob were going to make sure everyone kept a very level head. Work was done to protect the town as more barricades were made. Women helped make meals, and children were encouraged to play in the town hall side yard where the school children often enjoyed a break. Everyone was certainly helping, and it was unlike anything Tanner had ever seen before. The whole town of Bear Creek and the surrounding area were really coming together.

As the morning progressed into afternoon, the Sioux tribe came down from the mountains, men, women, and even children, to help the people of Bear Creek. Food was brought so everyone could have a meal. Teepees were constructed around the town so warriors and others from the tribe would have a place to sleep in order to do their part to help protect the area. It was such an outpouring of supplies and hope that for once

Tanner wasn't afraid of being around so many Indians. Everyone was smiling and feeling such relief that the Sioux had arrived to help them, feeling that there was no need to fear anything.

After eating some of the Indian stew that had been prepared with bits of fry bread, Tanner went looking for Bethany. He smiled as he found her behind the inn with a dozen other women, all working hard to do the laundry. It was as though this area of town had been designated for washing and cleaning, and the person who seemed to be heading it all was Matilda as she stood amongst all the ladies and delegated the work. He was glad to see the young lady was finding her place amongst the community.

Hanging clean clothes on the line was Bethany, looking radiant in the afternoon sun. It made her blonde hair seem even more golden. Tanner slowly approached, taking the time to really observe Bethany without her noticing. She was wearing a crème colored cotton gown, which was good for the work she was helping with, but still a finer quality than any of the other women around her. But it was not her clothes that helped her to stand out. It was her positive attitude despite all the danger they were currently facing.

"Hi there, Bethany," Tanner said when he was getting close. He didn't want to scare her while she was working and accidently drop a clean cloth on the ground to only wash it once more.

"Hi, Tanner," Bethany replied with a bright smile as she finished pinning the garment and turned towards him. She dried her hands on her apron, and though she was new to work she had taken to it like a fish to water.

"It seems that Miss Rayford's cleaning business has really taken off," Tanner said as he gestured towards the other woman.

"My word, there is plenty of washing to be done. Thankfully, with so many people in town, there are many able hands. There have been many Indian women in and out of the kitchen as well to help cook for everyone. It's quite a sight," she said happily.

"There was not great news this morning," Tanner said. "These outlaws are really trying to scare people and confuse us all. It seems we'll have to wait for them to bring the fight to us."

"That sounds rather dangerous for a lot of people," Bethany said, her smile fading. He hated to see her concerned or afraid. But that was the reality of the situation. Everyone was nervous about the unknowns when it came to these outlaws.

"It's not ideal, that's for sure. But the Sioux are many, and they are here in town to help us. I even heard that the Indian warriors are going to perch themselves on top of all the buildings so they can keep watch in the night for anyone trying to sneak into town," Tanner explained.

"Well, I suppose I should be reassured by the number of able people instead of being afraid," Bethany said.

"I won't let anything happen to you," Tanner said, reaching for her hand. Bethany allowed him to take her hand, and for a moment they just stood together and enjoyed the feeling of holding hands. Tanner smiled at Bethany, thinking how he couldn't wait for them to marry and start a family together. He was so happy that Bethany had been the one he had replied to and who had come out to see him. It filled him with so much excitement and happiness that just for a moment he could forget about all the troubles that surrounded them.

"Well, I won't keep you long," Tanner said after a while. "Did you get something to eat today?" He let go of Bethany's hand and she nodded.

"Yes, there is quite a bit of food to partake of," she said, her smile returning. "I was even able to try some of the Indian dishes and found them to be very good."

"I'm glad to hear. I'll come visit with you later in the day. Just have to keep on top of things and be available where the most help is needed."

"Of course. I completely understand," Bethany said.

They parted ways then, and Tanner made his way back around to the front of the inn. He surveyed the area around him, really seeing how everyone was working hard to not only prepare for these outlaws, but to also support one another. He heard laughter on the wind and knew that at least the people of Bear Creek were still keeping up their spirits. No one was outright panicking or trying to convince others to try to run away. There was a complete unity that made Tanner proud to be a part of Bear Creek.

"Hey, Tanner!" called Jacob as he stood on the porch of the clinic. Tanner quickly made his way over to the Sheriff, seeing the look of concern on his face. "I just talked to one of the Peters boys. He swears he saw a small group of women on the edge of the farm when he was trying to fight the fire with his brother and father. He had the thought to try to signal them for help, but he became so focused on the fire he lost track of them."

“A group of women? That sounds rather strange,” Tanner agreed as he raised his hand and started to rub his chin. “Why would a group of women have anything to do with this?”

“Do you think they could be working for the outlaws? None of the reports said anything about women being numbered with the outlaws.”

“Reports wouldn’t have details on the women if no one knew that they were a part of all this madness. You don’t… you don’t think that’s how they do it? They send a group of women to spy out in the area and give the details back to the outlaws so they know how to hit a town just perfectly?” Tanner asked, his nervousness seeming to return.

“Seen any strange women in town?” Jacob asked as they both turned towards the street, a crowd of people moving back and forth to attend to different tasks.

“No. Only because I wasn’t looking,” Tanner said, his eyes darting in every direction to see if he noticed anyone unfamiliar.

“Well, let’s head out and see if we spot any women we don’t know. Between the two of us, we should be able to spot something,” Jacob said, lowering his voice. Tanner nodded to his boss and set out, determined to find any spies amongst them.

CHAPTER 19

Bethany had to admit she was grateful that at least she was in a town full of people when danger was near. It was all scary to think about what could possibly happen. She sometimes imagined the town she was starting to love being overcome by men who wished to do harm to property and people. She had heard about what happened to the Peters' farm and how the poor men had been burned while trying to save their home. Bethany didn't like the idea of that happening to anyone else.

Despite all that was happening in town, Bethany didn't regret coming to Bear Creek one bit. She was enjoying her work with Matilda, and especially seeing how Matilda was taking a great leadership role to help the women stay organized and to keep the progress of the wash going. Bethany could easily see her as a business owner and hoped that one day her dream would come true. Bethany certainly had hope that one day soon life in Bear Creek would return to some sort of normal, and she and Matilda would really get to start their new life fully.

Bethany had just picked up another basket of clean clothes to hang on the line when she noticed Tanner on the other side of the clothesline. At first, she thought he'd been trying to sneak up on her and perhaps surprise her. She almost said hello to him when he quickly raised his finger and pressed it to his lips. Bethany was confused, but he motioned for her to come a bit closer.

"Don't be afraid," he said softly. "Do you recognize any of the women helping you and Matilda wash from last night? The ones I introduced you to?" Bethany thought about his question and ended up shaking her head. She and Matilda weren't familiar with any of the women and were just happy for the help.

"Alright, you just keep doing what you're doing. I'm going to go get the sheriff. Whatever you do, don't let anyone know I was here. Not even Matilda," Tanner said in a soft voice. "I'll tell you more later." Bethany just nodded her head, trusting the man. She then returned to hanging the laundry as Tanner slipped away between the clothes and out around the inn.

Bethany was sure curious to know what was going on. She looked at the group of women she'd been working with all morning, careful not to stare. She was curious about them then, wondering why they had been of interest to Tanner. Trying to push the thoughts out of her mind, she focused only on hanging the laundry and doing a good job to help the people who needed clean clothes when they didn't have the means to do so since they were now living in town.

Bethany had just grabbed another basket of freshly cleaned clothes when several Sioux Indians came walking behind the inn. They came from the open side, the back of the inn through the kitchen, the way that Tanner had come. She instantly stilled as they were soon surrounded by Indians. No one said a word as everything became very silent. Bethany looked around and noticed about a group of six women all looking at one another as though they weren't sure what to do.

Then, the sheriff and Tanner came through the circle of Indians, looking straight at the group of six women. Bethany moved to Matilda's side, pulling her close to her and out of everyone's way. She studied the faces of the six women, all of them wearing white bonnets that helped shade their faces from the sun. They wore simple gowns of cotton and didn't look any different than any other woman Bethany had met in Bear Creek so far. All morning everyone had worked well together and even had a good time sharing stories and good jokes.

"Ladies, who are you with?" the sheriff asked as he placed his hand on his hips.

"We are Freda's daughters," one woman said. She looked to be the oldest out of all of them and proudly stood tall with her shoulders back.

"I don't know any Freda around here," the sheriff replied. "What are you doing in Bear Creek?" The women started to look around as they clambered together, but the Indians stepped forward, blocking all paths of escape. The sight of it all made Bethany very nervous.

"That is because Freda isn't from around here. Yet, it is no less the truth," the woman replied. Bethany detected an accent then, one she wasn't familiar with.

"That does not explain why you are here," the sheriff pressed.

"We are here for work." The woman gestured towards the wash they had been doing all day. "We are good workers and want to earn some coin." Bethany watched as the sheriff looked at them for a good two minutes as silence took hold once more. Then he gestured towards the Indians, waving his hand in a circular motion that looked to Bethany to mean to round them all up.

"Let's take them to the jail," the sheriff said over the commotion of the women talking quickly in a language Bethany had never heard before. They started to shout with one another, and then at the sheriff. But it didn't matter what any of them said. The Indians were quick to secure each one by the arms, leading them quickly from behind the inn towards the other part of town. All Bethany could do was watch in shock as the scene unfolded in front of her. When the washing area behind the inn quieted down once more, Tanner came walking towards the pair of them.

"Sorry you two had to witness that," Tanner said with a sigh. "We learned from one of the Peters boys that they had seen a group of women not too far away from their farm when they were fighting the house fire. Got a hunch and had to follow through with it."

"What does this have to do with the outlaws?" Bethany asked as she finally let go of Matilda's hand, feeling calm once more.

"We're thinking this might be one of the ways the outlaws are able to cripple towns so quickly. They have a small group of women go into town, disguised as someone else to learn as much as they can and relay the information to the outlaws. If these women were already in town, that means the outlaws can't be too far away," Tanner explained.

"We didn't know," Matilda confessed. "They were all working so hard that I didn't even think that they weren't from around here. Their accents were strange, but that was all. I wasn't going to judge."

"No one is going to blame you, Matilda," Tanner said with a soft smile. "You two are new here and wouldn't have ever known. They may have found that out and stuck by your side because they wouldn't be talked about with anyone else. But I thought they looked strange when I visited earlier. Gut feelings are always things to trust."

"I'll have to keep that in mind," Bethany said, thinking her gut was telling her good things about Tanner. He was obviously very smart and quick on his feet. He was certainly the type of man that Bethany could be proud to say was her husband.

"Alright ladies, I'll leave you two for the time being. Sorry we had to gather up all your help," Tanner said as he nodded to them both before hurrying off towards the sheriff's office.

Bethany sighed as she looked around at all the laundry that still needed to be done. It would be a hard task for just her and Matilda to accomplish. But, knowing how many people were counting on them, Bethany didn't complain as they got to work.

"What language do you think those women were speaking?" Matilda asked as she sat on a stool and started to scrub a pair of trousers on the wash board.

"I'm not sure," Bethany said as she started to wring the

water from the clean clothes that had been soaking in the soapy water. Once they were mostly wrung out, she would go and hang them up. "I've heard a few different languages during parties. French. Italian. British and Irish accents. But what I heard from those women was nothing like I've heard in the past."

"I have a bad feeling about all of this," Matilda said with a sigh. "It's like they are people from very far away that think what they are doing is right. That's all I can reason about this whole situation."

"They must be very sick in the head if they think killing and burning homes is the right thing to do," Bethany said, afraid to even say such things out loud. She had no idea what would convince a person to do such a thing, and to think there was a large group of them all working together. It was such a grotesque situation that Bethany didn't like to even contemplate the reasoning behind it all because it almost scared her more than the reality of the dangers they faced.

For the rest of the day, Bethany simply focused on the wash. She felt proud of all she was able to accomplish when families came to pick up their clean clothes at sundown. Bethany wasn't sure how they had done it after losing so many helpers, but they had finished all the laundry together. It was such a great feeling to see the happy families as they left with their clean clothes. To Bethany, it seemed like a small service. But it seemed to all the people they had helped that it meant the world to them to have clean clothes.

Matilda was probably the happier of the two of them because of all the money she had earned by doing the work. "I don't think there is much of anything to buy in Bear Creek besides the things you really need, like food. But I like to think that if we were back in Tennessee, I would take us out to dinner at a fine restaurant, sporting our nicest gowns."

"That's very nice of you to say," Bethany said, even though she didn't like to be reminded of where they had come from. Even with all the danger and mystery surrounding them, she still thought her current situation was far better than the one she'd left.

CHAPTER 20

Tanner made it to the jail just in time to watch Jacob start his interrogation. He was very curious to know more about these women and how they had been able to sneak into town without anyone realizing they were new. Especially since Bear Creek was a very small town and everyone knew everyone. A pair of Indians remained in the jail with Tanner and Jacob as the six women were gathered together in one of the three jail cells.

"Alright, let's make this quick. What are you doing in this town?" Jacob asked. Tanner heard the women whispering to each other in a language he didn't recognize at all. When the women didn't say anything, Jacob repeated the question. But the only person the women were talking to were each other.

"Do you know what they're saying?" Jacob asked one of the Indians standing nearby. But the Indians only shook their heads.

"This is not an Indian language," the warrior said. "It is like a white language from far away."

"What do you mean?" Jacob asked.

"From a place the white man came from," the Indian answered. "Look at their very white skin and blonde hair. They are very white." Jacob and Tanner both pressed their faces up against the iron bars to get a good look at the women. They both realized that the Indian was right. They all had blonde hair and blue eyes. The more Tanner thought about it, the more an idea came to mind.

"German," Tanner said, speaking up so the women could hear him. They stopped talking and looked at him as though waiting for something to happen.

"France," Tanner then tried. Still no answer.

"Norway…" Still no response.

"Dutch!" Tanner's raised voice seemed to startle them, or perhaps it was the word he said. They started to all whine and moan as though they were in pain. Or, maybe they had become very afraid. "I would say they're from the Netherlands, Boss. They speak Dutch there, and it's close to the ancient places of fair-faced people."

"How in the world do you know such things, Tanner?" Jacob asked, completely perplexed.

"I suppose I just like to read about history," Tanner said with a shrug. "My father used to tell me wild stories about Vikings when I was little, and the Netherlands was a place the Vikings tried to fight the Dutch. I read all I could about it when my father would get his hands on a new history book."

"Tanner, you never cease to surprise me," Jacob said as he

turned back to the women. "Alright, who wants to tell me why a bunch of Dutch women are all the way in Montana?"

"Because we had to," came a stressed voice from one of the women, her accent very thick. She left her friends and approached the iron bars, a look of dread on her face. She was called back by another woman, but she didn't listen to her.

"We were forced from our homes and brought to this place. Told to serve the men that bought us," she explained. Tanner felt a sense of dread wash over him at the woman's words. "We have no choice. But now…I don't want to see no more death."

"Who are the men that bought you?" Jacob asked, his voice steady.

"They are men who think they are gods, sent here to purge the land of all sinners. They enslave many to do their bidding. But it is the three brothers that lead them, keep the slaves worshiping them as gods," she said, her voice cracking as tears filled her eyes. "But they are not gods. I see that now… they are monsters." Tears slid from her eyes then, and Tanner felt bad for these women.

"Boss, I got a very bad feeling about this," Tanner whispered towards Jacob. The sheriff nodded in reply. Tanner felt he was about to learn something dreadful he'd be happier to never hear.

"Miss, how about you start from the beginning. You tell me your whole story, and I promise to protect you," Jacob said. She quickly dried her tears then, rubbing her face on her gown sleeve.

"No one can stop them," she said.

"But we have a whole tribe of Indians on our side," Jacob

said, gesturing towards the two Indian warriors still in the jail with them. "We outnumber those forty outlaws." She didn't look convinced as she looked from Jacob to the Indians.

"They have Indians, too," she said. "Ones who drink the blood of their enemies." Tanner shivered at the thought. It brought back too many painful memories, and he almost fled from the jail at the very mention of it.

"The more you tell us, the more we'll be able to protect you," Jacob said, trying to speak softly to the women. She stared at Jacob for a long time, but eventually nodded. The other women didn't seem to like what was happening, and they whispered back and forth between each other, a look of terror on of their faces.

"We were told that if we ever found ourselves in this situation, that it would be better to kill ourselves than to be taken hostage," she said as she sat upon the wooden bench of the jail. Jacob sat down as well, Tanner following suit. They sat cross-legged as they gave the woman their full attention. "But I don't want to die."

"We're not going to hurt you," Jacob said. "Even when you tell us your story, we'd rather help you all than cause you more harm."

"As you were told earlier, we are Freda's daughters. Freda was our mother back in the Netherlands. When our mother passed away, our father sold us into slavery to supply his drinking habit. One day, about a year after becoming slaves, we were purchased by men of the Americas and sent on a ship to meet these men. Those months at sea were horrible.

"Yet not as horrible as what we experienced in America. The three brothers showered us with affection, gowns, and even jewels. We thought we were brides fit for kings. But we soon learned that it was all for show. We were taught to sneak into places and learn knowledge for the three brothers. Then, they used that knowledge and commanded their army to kill, and burn, and steal."

The woman shuddered as though remembering everything she had witnessed at that moment. She hugged her arms around her body as though trying to fight off a cold wind that suddenly swept through the jail. But the building was warm since it had no windows for fresh air.

"For five years we did this, me and my sisters. At first, it was just a farm or a nice house the brothers went after. But after a few years, their following grew. Men wanted to be like the brothers, to be wealthy and take whatever they wanted. These hungry, greedy men wanted to be with fine ladies like me and my sisters. And when the three brothers had their army, they started killing everyone and everything in sight, convincing the men that they were gods cleansing the earth of sin."

Jacob shook his head as the woman fell silent and lowered her head. Tanner could hardly believe what had been said. It was such a dark and gruesome story that it was certainly difficult to comprehend. How could three men have so much power and control over so many? How had no one put a stop to this before? All that Tanner could reason was that no one had any real idea of what had really happened. And now that they had the women, these three brothers wouldn't have the information they needed to have an advantage over the town. Thankfully, Jacob and Tanner could convince the women to share as many details as possible.

"Please tell us more about the Indians?" one of the warriors asked, coming to sit in front of the bars as well.

"Captured Blackfoot Indians, treated like dogs. Forced to be sneaky and set fires," the women explained. Tanner noticed the grief-stricken expression on the Indian's face.

"I must go tell my Chief. These Indians must be rescued from slavery," the warrior said as his fellow Indian helped him stand. Together, they quickly left the jail.

"How many men do the brothers have?" Tanner asked.

"It is hard to know the true number. But I have been forced to lay with twenty-six different men," she confessed, a look of shame on her face. Tanner heard Jacob curse underneath his breath. They both understood now that these women weren't being used just to gather information. They were used for pleasure against their will to satisfy the lusts of men.

"How do these brothers destroy so many towns so quick, with no one being able to stop them?" Jacob asked, the ultimate question finally being spoken out loud.

"They are very sneaky," the woman said, looking up at Jacob. "They first send us. We then give them the information. Then, the Indians come, setting fire to everything. When the people try to run and flee, they are struck down by the mountain men. Then the brothers come, shooting their guns and stealing all the things they need."

"Do you know where they are now?" Tanner asked, feeling his heart pound in his chest.

"No, we do not. We are waiting for the messenger to come and take us back," the woman explained. "He is a man like us, speaking our language. He will know where they are."

"What do you all need?" Jacob asked.

"Food and water. A place to sleep. This jail may be the safest place for us," the woman said as she looked around the space. "Though the wood would burn us alive. It might be a fitting end for what we've done."

"We will get you the things you need," Jacob said. "But I promise to protect you all." The woman said nothing as she stood and joined her sisters. She began to talk to them in their language, and what she said did not appear to make them happy at all. There was much arguing, and Tanner watched as one of the women slapped the one who had told them everything. But the woman did not look like she regretted anything as she rubbed her cheek and stared at the one who had hit her, quieting all the rest of them.

When Tanner and Jacob were certain that the women weren't going to tear each other apart, they stepped outside of the jail, cool air coming to greet them. They looked around at the town, the bustling of the people as everyone worked together to prepare. But in the back of Tanner's mind, he wondered if any of their preparations would make a difference against the brutality that was heading their way.

"I feel as though I'm not quite sure what to do," Jacob said, his voice very soft and low. Tanner looked at him, seeing the shock on the sheriff's face. "I've never dealt with anything like this, nor could I have imagined such a terrifying story."

"I don't think anything in life could have prepared us, Boss," Tanner said, letting out a deep sigh. "We need to let the mayor know what we've learned and to be on the lookout for this Dutch fellow who is supposed to come into town and collect the women. He'll know where the outlaws are."

"Yeah, I suppose you are right," Jacob said. He took off

his hat and ran his fingers through his hair. "Let's go give everyone an update, then get these women some food and water. They've been through enough hell as it is." Tanner nodded his agreement as they set off towards town hall, uneasy about having to repeat such a dreadful story.

CHAPTER 21

Bethany was sitting at a dining table outside the inn, the sun having set. Matilda had gone off to bed early, stating how tired she'd become. Bethany didn't blame her because they had all worked very hard that day to do all the wash. And if things continued as they were, they would have more wash to do tomorrow as well. But Bethany was still hoping she'd have a chance to meet with Tanner. With a candle burning on the table before her, she waited for the deputy to make an appearance.

When she was the only one occupying a table outside the inn, she figured it was time she went inside and got some sleep herself. Most of the town had settled for the night, and she didn't like the idea of being outside alone. She stood and picked up the candle from the table, making sure to push in her chair on the grass lawn before making her way towards the main door to the inn.

She reached for the door handle just as she heard her name

being called. She turned to see Tanner jogging over towards her, looking quite out of breath. Bethany smiled as she stepped away from the door and approached him, carrying the candle close to her body so the wind wouldn't blow it out.

"I wondered if I would see you tonight. Been in meetings all afternoon and had only hoped you'd still be awake," Tanner explained as he caught his breath.

"I was just heading inside," Bethany admitted. "But I'm glad I got to see you before I went off to bed."

"Sorry for keeping you," Tanner said. "It's been such a bizarre afternoon that I thought just getting to talk with you would help me feel better."

"Oh? What's been going on?" Bethany asked, sad to hear how he was feeling.

"Honestly, it's a pretty gruesome story. We learned more about the women and it's so terrible that I wouldn't want to share it with you. No doubt you'd have nightmares tonight," Tanner explained, resting his hands on his hips.

"Really? That terrible?" Bethany asked. She then gestured to the nearest table and chairs, and they both took a seat as Bethany placed the candle on the table.

"It's a story that nightmares are made of," Tanner said as he ran his fingers through his brown hair. Bethany didn't like to see him so stressed. She reached across the table and took his hand in hers, holding it tight. "This feels good."

"Yeah, it sure does," she replied. They sat like that for a little while, enjoying the evening breeze. An owl hooted in the distance and Bethany turned her head towards the sound, having never heard an owl call before. She smiled, thinking it was a lovely sound that echoed in the distance.

"It's hard to think Bear Creek is in danger when it feels so peaceful right now," Bethany said as she turned her eyes back on Tanner. She blushed when she realized he'd been watching her that entire time.

"I feel peaceful when I'm with you," Tanner confessed. "There is so much raging on around us, but when I sit here and hold your hand I feel at ease."

"The women earlier. What happened to them?" Bethany asked. She didn't want to disturb his peaceful moment, but she was curious to know what had happened in town since she'd last seen him.

Tanner nodded as he sighed once more. Then he said, "It turns out that those women sort of work for the outlaws, sneaking into towns and gathering information. Only, they are forced to do so. They were taken from their homes and given a very terrible life."

"That's awful," Bethany said as she stilled, placing her hand over her heart. "I can't imagine being forced to do such a thing."

"Those women have been through a lot of hard times," Tanner explained. "But we are going to protect them from the outlaws now that we've been able to find them out and learn why they've been doing this. One of them has been rather helpful, and it all makes sense now why none of the other towns in Montana have been successful at fighting them off."

"Do you think that there is anything Matilda and I could possibly do for them?" Bethany asked. Tanner rubbed his chin, thinking about it for a moment.

"Well, how did they seem to be when they were helping with the wash?" he asked.

"They seemed happy as can be. That is why I thought it was so strange when you and the sheriff came for them. They seemed to be acting like normal women," Bethany said honestly.

"I think when this is all over, there is going to be six women who are going to be looking to start over with their lives. They might be of help to Matilda with this washing business she's wanting to start up," Tanner suggested. "However, until the outlaws can be dealt with, it's best to keep them in the jail for their own safety."

"I'm sure a jail isn't much better than what these women have been through," Bethany said, wishing something could be done now for them.

"Really, it's in their best interest. Safest place in Bear Creek besides the Sioux camp up in the mountains," Tanner said.

"If that's the case, why don't all the women and children make their way up there now?" Bethany asked.

"You know, we've thought about that before. I think tomorrow when I check in with the sheriff and the mayor I'll bring that point up to them again. Things are starting to get serious now that we understand how these outlaws work. If we can fool them into thinking we don't know anything, we might be able to be the ones to surprise them in the end," Tanner said, a small grin forming on his face. "I think you and I work well together."

"Oh, I was just thinking out loud," Bethany said, a deep blush forming on her cheeks. "That's all."

"Don't be so modest. It's good to know you think for yourself, and others," Tanner said as he squeezed her hand then let it go. "Well, I best be heading home. Need to get some sleep before morning comes."

"Of course. I shouldn't have kept you so long," Bethany said as she picked up the candle, wanting to make sure it was returned to the inn.

"You didn't keep me at all," Tanner said reassuringly. "I wanted to see you and get to visit with you a bit. And now I have." He leaned forward and placed a short kiss on her cheek. She blushed again, thinking how nice it was to be shown affection by a man who actually cared about her. They said their goodbyes then and Bethany went into the inn, feeling as though everything would one day be perfectly okay.

The inn was relatively quiet despite all the people sleeping in the dining room. Bethany made sure not to make a peep as she crossed the entryway, walked past the counter, and down the first-floor hallway. As she came to her shared room with Matilda, she used the room key to enter, finding the room already in darkness. Bethany shut the door behind her as she entered the room, hearing Matilda's soft snores as she did so. She made quick work of getting ready for bed, and once she had snuffed the candle, got slowly into bed so as not to wake her friend.

As Bethany pulled the covers up over her, she nestled down into the bed and against her pillow. She thought about all the things she knew she should be grateful for despite the dangers the town was facing. She was in a nice bed, her best friend by her side. A sturdy roof was over their heads, and they had been able to enjoy three hardy meals that day. Matilda seemed to have the beginnings of a successful washing business. And each day that passed helped Bethany to see just how wonderful Tanner was as a deputy, and all the potential he had as her future husband.

The very thought of marrying Tanner one day in the near future caused Bethany to smile brightly in the darkness of the room. It was exciting to think she'd be marrying a man she was proud of, who she knew would take good care of her, and more importantly, someone she was convinced she'd be able to fall in love with. He'd been very attentive of her even though he was being pulled in many directions to do his job as a deputy. The fact that he was taking time out of his day to visit with her really meant a lot to her.

Eventually, Bethany closed her eyes to the shadows dancing across the wall from the swaying tree in the wind outside the window. She pictured in her mind what it would be like to be married to Tanner. Bethany dreamed of her family that she would one day have with Tanner. And as her mind wandered from fantasy to fantasy, she eventually took her thoughts into a bliss-filled dream.

CHAPTER 22

The major downside of having all the folks of Bear Creek nestled in one area was that news traveled fast. By the time Tanner made it into town that morning and headed straight for the sheriff's office, he encountered a small mob out front as a group of men faced the sheriff on the porch. Jacob had his arms crossed over his chest, his eyes narrowed at the man in front of him, who seemed to be leading the group of angry-looking townsfolk. At least Tanner could see plenty of familiar faces.

"They should be hung for what they've done to other towns," cried the man in the front.

"The men who forced those women to do cruel things should be hung," Jacob called back. "They've been stolen from their homes, sold into slavery, and raped countless times. So how about you all return to your darn business and leave the law to me?" Tanner had never seen Jacob worked up so bad in his life, and as his anger showed on his face, so did the same on the faces of those gathered. There was mumbling in the group before the men started to disperse. The man who had started the ruckus in the first place, Mr. Miller, walked away with his head hung low.

"Sounds like you've had an eventful morning," Tanner said as he finished leading his horse forward. He slipped off the saddle and tethered his horse at the hitching post, thinking he'd take the gelding to the livery stables later on.

"I just can't stand it when everyday folk think they know how to do my job," Jacob huffed. "We got more important things to worry about than our own causing trouble." Jacob shook his head and went into the office with Tanner closely behind him.

"I was thinking last night that perhaps we should encourage all the women and children to head up the mountain to the Sioux camp," Tanner said as Jacob went over to the wood stove and poured himself a cup of hot coffee from the kettle. The sheriff blew on it a few times before taking a sip, but he nodded his head nonetheless.

"If what this Dutch woman has said is true, then the next step in the outlaws' plan is to bring the six sisters back to their location before attacking. It would be smart to get all of those who can't fight to the camp. At least up there, they'll be far from the fight without any of us having to worry about them becoming a target," Jacob reasoned.

"I was hoping you had the same line of thought as me," Tanner said. "I'm sure once we tell the mayor and Brown Bear, they will agree as well."

"Yeah, especially after one of the Indian scouts reported that two more farms have been burned down. They are closer to town, so it's only a matter of time before these outlaws try to strike."

"That's why I think it's time that we do all we can to fool these outlaws, make them think one thing while leading them all into a trap," Tanner said. "If the sisters went back to the outlaws and told them the wrong information, it would be greatly to our advantage."

"Tanner, I don't like the sound of that," Jacob said with a sigh. "I told those women that we would protect them. I doubt they'll like the idea of being used as bait. They've already been used enough."

"I know, Jacob. And I completely get what you are saying. However, this may be our only way to outsmart these outlaws. I think the sisters would like the idea because it will give them control over the situation and a way to finally get some payback on their captors. We'll give them enough information so they can find their way back to Bear Creek if the outlaws are too far from town for them to remember."

Jacob sipped his coffee slowly, thinking deeply about Tanner's plan. It would give them a great advantage if the six sisters were willing to work for them. But it would also be very risky. Something might happen to the women before Jacob could make sure they were safe again. And the women might tell their captives everything and only make it harder for Bear Creek to defend itself.

"It won't hurt to at least talk to them about it," Jacob eventually said once he was finished with his coffee. "Might as well head over there now to speak with them and make sure someone has brought them some breakfast."

Tanner nodded his agreement and followed his boss from

the building. Together they walked the short distance to the jail next door. Inside the jail they found the women eating together, still bunched up in the corner as they looked around in fear. He hated to see them this way and to know how terrible they had been treated for so long.

"Good morning," Jacob said to the group, but no one replied as they all eyed the sheriff with fear in their eyes. "We came up with a plan on how to stop these outlaws once and for all. But we are going to need your help."

"What do you need from us?" asked the woman who had confessed all the details the day before. She stood from where she'd been eating and came closer to the iron bars.

"I understand that someone will be coming for all of you soon to take you back to the brothers to tell them everything you know about our town. If you are willing to lie to them, to give them false information, then we would be able to surprise them and take them all down," Jacob explained. Tanner watched as the woman's eyebrows furrowed in confusion. It took her several moments to respond.

"It will be hard to offer your protection to us if we go back to them," she said. "The three brothers stay back and do not let us out of their sight when the fighting begins."

"What would draw them out and convince them to join in the fight?" Tanner asked, stepping forward.

The woman thought about it for a moment before saying, "Money and gold. If they know there is a lot of it, they will come personally to protect it from their men."

"Then I have the perfect idea," Tanner said. "Tell the brothers that the bank has loads of cash and gold because of the miners here in Bear Creek. Explain that the men are old and worn from working the mines. That it will be easy for them to take us all out."

"And what about us?" the woman was quick to reply.

"We will make sure you know how to reach Bear Creek, no matter where this outlaw camp is. We want you all to make it safely back here. And if you don't show up after the fighting is over, then we'll come searching for you," Jacob said, completely meaning every single word he spoke.

The woman didn't respond to Jacob right away. She went back to her sisters and knelt before them, speaking softly in their home language. As Tanner watched, he saw the fear in their eyes grow. He could tell that none of them liked the idea of going back to their captors. But the woman persisted. She talked softly, looking to do her best to comfort them and reassure each and every one of them that this was in their best interest. And hopefully, she included plenty of details of how this would lead to the demise of the three brothers and they would finally have their revenge.

Eventually, when the sisters all seemed calm once more, the woman returned to the iron bars and nodded. "We will do this thing you have asked of us," she said. "Only because we would like to know that these men would be finally stopped once and for all."

"Thank you," Jacob said. Tanner felt relieved, knowing that this had to go smoothly, or it would be all for nothing. "What is your name?"

"You may call me Samantha. It is a name I have grown fond of, and it has no ties to my past," she explained.

"Very well, Samantha. I look forward to doing business with you and getting you and your sisters all settled here in

Bear Creek when this is over," Jacob said, getting ready to depart. They had much to share with the others.

"What will we get in return?" Samantha asked before they could leave.

"Well, what is it that you want?" Jacob asked, turning back to the iron bars.

"A roof over our heads every night," Samantha said, grasping the bars with both hands. "A place to call our own. Decent food in our bellies. A clean place to sleep. And protection from men who would try to take advantage of us again."

"That's a reasonable enough request. There are a lot of good people here in Bear Creek. And once everyone learns it was you six that helped save this town, there is going to be a lot of folks who'd be happy to help," Jacob said.

"So, when do we get out of this jail then?" Samantha asked.

"Once we talk over this plan with the other officials, we'll let you go so you can deliver the message back to those men. Then, we'll be ready for their attack," Jacob explained. Samantha let go of the bars and went back to her food, talking lightly with her sisters. Tanner followed Jacob out of the jail, feeling a mix of emotions. He was sure this plan would work as long as they could actually trust these sisters.

"Seems they've started the morning meeting without us," Jacob said, pulling Tanner from his thoughts. Tanner looked ahead towards the town hall, seeing that the mayor and Brown Bear were already speaking with one another as a group of people gathered about.

"We can't lose all the farms!" came a man's voice. It was the eldest Peters boy, wrapped in bandages from his face to his leg. The sight of him made Tanner's stomach tighten. He felt terrible for all the families that had lost something so far.

"That's why we're going to lead them straight into a trap!" Jacob yelled back. "I bet by even tonight they'll be upon us, ready to strike. But we've found a way to manipulate them so we'll be ready for them and surprise them." Murmurs followed the sheriff's words as the crowd parted to let the two of them through to the center.

"What sort of plan?" Mayor Franklin asked.

"A secret one?" the sheriff said with a wink. "But we think that the women and children, and all those unable to fight, should head up to the Sioux camp to wait out this fight. I feel they would only get hurt."

"My people would be happy to accept these women and children, and tend to their needs," Brown Bear was quick to say. "The journey to camp is not too long on foot."

"Thank you, Brown Bear. It is important that we clear the town of all unnecessary people so there are not a lot of casualties," Jacob said.

"Not everyone is going to like this idea," said someone from the crowd. "We might be peaceful with the Indians, but the idea of living with them won't sit easily with some women."

"It's for their protection," Tanner spoke up. "I'll be the first one to admit that I'm quite nervous around Indians because of my past. But I'd trust Brown Bear and his people with my wife and children." More murmuring continued, but no one argued with what had been said.

"Alright folks, you've heard the official word. Let's help all the women and children make the journey up to the Sioux camp to get settled. Then, all those who are able to fire a gun or bow and arrow will meet back here at the town hall this evening to review our plan of attack. I'll be damned if I'll let this town fall to outlaws," Jacob said, his words causing the crowd around them to respond with cheers and applause. Everyone dispersed as the news of what they'd do next spread.

Tanner knew that he wanted to talk with Bethany before she went up to the camp. He waited for the morning meeting to be finished so he could hurry over to the inn and perhaps even help her and Matilda get ready for the journey up to the camp.

"Gentlemen, let's take this meeting into my office," the mayor said, gesturing over his shoulder with his thumb extended towards the town hall. They all followed after the man until they were situated in his office. Brown Bear was a tall man and his head almost touched the ceiling. Jacob settled into a chair in front of the mayor's desk, but Tanner was quite alright with just standing.

"The six sisters have agreed to help us," Jacob explained. "The one that speaks the most with us, Samantha, said that they are willing to give their slave owners false information that will benefit us. We'll be ready for their attack now that we understand how they work."

"Can we trust them?" the mayor asked.

"They are eager to be free of these men, and no doubt seek a little revenge on them as well. They only ask for basic things in return. A roof over their heads. A clean place to sleep every night. Decent food to eat. It's so sad that all I can think is that these women have truly been through hell," Jacob said, his voice strained. Tanner could tell that this situation was really affecting him. No one liked the idea of women being used and abused for personal gain.

"Then what will happen next with the women? How will they know how to find these outlaws to tell their false story?" Brown Bear asked.

"Samantha explained that someone will come into town and gather them up. This person will lead them back to the outlaws and prepare for a swift attack," Jacob said.

"Then I shall send my best trackers to follow after them, to know where these outlaws are. And they will make sure that the women are watched over," Brown Bear said. "Gentlemen, I would also like to talk to you about the Blackfoot Indians that have been captured and used as slaves as well. If there is a chance that they could be rescued and brought into my tribe to live peaceful lives, I would like to act upon it."

"Brown Bear, are these Indians the type you'd want in your tribe? Samantha said they drink the blood of their enemies," Jacob said.

"It is a very old tradition, I will not deny that. But if there is a way I could save them, I would like to try," Brown Bear said, his stern chief voice coming out.

"I trust you, Brown Bear. You may act as you see fit. I know you will not let others be harmed to save these Indians," the mayor agreed.

"Thank you," Brown Bear said with a grunt of approval.

"Well then, there is a lot of work that needs to be done today. Let's get these women and children to camp, and start putting a plan together for these men," the mayor said, his words causing the meeting to come to an end. Tanner took that as his cue to see Bethany while he still could.

CHAPTER 23

When Mr. Tibet came to Bethany and Matilda's room in the morning, at first Bethany thought the inn owner was just coming to let them know that breakfast was being served. But when he said that all women and children would be heading up the mountain to the Sioux camp, she was shocked.

"What has happened to cause such an order from the sheriff and mayor?" Matilda asked. She would no doubt be upset about not being able to operate her cleaning business that morning.

"The word is trouble is headed straight for us and it's best that those who can't fight go somewhere safe 'til these outlaws can be taken care of," Mr. Tibet explained. "So I'd pack a small bag with enough supplies for a few days and come get some breakfast before we all head up the mountain."

Mr. Tibet let them be after that, shutting the door once more. Bethany and Matilda just looked at each other for a minute, both of them shocked by the news. Then, without saying a word, they started to pack up their things once more.

"Do you think we should try to take it all with us?" Matilda asked.

"We have two small trunks. I think we can manage, even if we have to carry them all day by ourselves," Bethany said.

Both of the women had just finished packing when another knock sounded on the door. This time Bethany answered it and was happy to see that Tanner was standing at the door. She smiled brightly at him, mostly because she couldn't help it. She was excited to see him.

"Seems you two got the message," Tanner said as he saw their trunks on the bed. "The first group of women and children are already making their way up the mountain. With so many families having moved into town, it won't take them much longer to gather their things once more and head up the wagon trail."

"Is it very far?" Matilda asked.

"It will take a good three hours on foot," Tanner said honestly. "It's best if you pack lightly."

"This is all we have," Bethany said, gesturing to the two trunks. "It won't be much for us to bear."

"Well, I'd be happy to help as well," Tanner said. "My next meeting isn't until this evening, so I'm free to go up the mountain with you."

"I'm sure we'd both appreciate the company," Bethany said, looking over her shoulder at Matilda. Her friend nodded in return.

"Alright. How about you two go get some breakfast and I'll bring my horse around. I'm sure we can secure at least one trunk to the saddle, and I'll do my best to carry the other," Tanner said.

"Don't worry, Deputy. We can all take turns," Matilda said as she closed her trunk and locked it. Tanner then went off to get his horse while Bethany and Matilda made quick work of eating a piece of toast with a fried egg on top. There were so many people in the breakfast line through the kitchen that Bethany was certain that Mrs. Tibet and her many helpers would soon run out of food. It was a hard thing to be feeding so many people. Yet they did the very best they could.

With some food in their bellies, Bethany and Matilda carried their trunks out of the inn and found Tanner standing a little way off with his horse. Tanner took Bethany's trunk and lifted it onto the back of his horse's saddle. He then secured it tightly before taking Matilda's trunk.

"Who wants to lead the horse by the reins?" he asked once they were all ready to follow the trail of people already leaving town and heading up the mountain path.

"I will try it," Bethany said, looking at the beautiful chestnut horse. She took the reins, holding them easily in her hands. After brushing back her blonde hair behind her ears, she felt ready to lead the horse.

Bethany found that the horse responded quite well to her and simply followed her lead. Tanner walked beside her as he carried the trunk, giving her small tips to improve her grip on the reins where she held them in her hands.

"You never want to wrap your fingers in the reins just in case the horse pulls back suddenly. That's a good way to get a bunch of broken fingers. Just hold it tightly in both hands and keep your hands near your hips. That way the horse knows to follow you and to stay focused on which way you are going," Tanner explained.

"Seems easy enough," Bethany said with a smile. The three of them followed the many other families that were leaving town and heading up the mountain trail. The further up they traveled, the more the forest came to surround them. Bethany realized it was much cooler in the mountains, surrounded by all the trees and foliage. She found it rather beautiful. And as they had to cross a stream, she enjoyed the sound of running water and the coolness of the breeze that ran over the water and danced around them.

"This place is so beautiful," Bethany said as she walked with her friends. Tanner had given Matilda a turn with the trunk, and she seemed to be bearing the weight without issue. For a stout woman, Matilda was quite strong.

"It is a nice place for a horse ride, especially in the summer when it gets pretty hot in town. But you always have to be careful of bears. I'm sure a group this size will cause enough noise to keep them away. But you never know when it comes to bears," Tanner warned.

"I'll be sure not to wander the forest alone then," Bethany said with a chuckle.

Bethany had a sense that after a few hours, they were coming closer to the Indian camp. The path that they were on started to widen, and there was much chatter up ahead of them along the trail. Eventually they came to a stop as a large crowd had gathered in one area, as though something was preventing them all from moving forward.

"I better go and see what the holdup is," Tanner said as he

quickly walked away from them and hurried around to address the crowd.

"You sure got yourself a fine fellow there," Matilda said as she came to stand next to Bethany. "I think any man willing to carry a woman's trunk this long is a good man." Bethany couldn't help but laugh freely at her friend's comment. Compared to the type of men they'd been exposed to in Tennessee, Tanner was certainly a breath of fresh air.

Eventually Tanner came back around to them as the crowd started to move once more. "As expected, not all the women are real keen about the idea of staying at the camp. There are plenty of available teepees since most of the tribe's men are down in the town. The women of the tribe are offering to take in families to their own teepees, and some of the town's folk were nervous. They seem to be all straightened out now," Tanner explained. "And I have a special friend who's agreed to take you two in."

Tanner took the reins from Bethany then, and she took Matilda's trunk to give her a break. The two women followed after Tanner as they cut through the Indian camp. Bethany was so intrigued by everything they were passing that it was hard to remain quiet and not ask a million questions. There was a sea of teepees as far as she could see. Indian women and children were everywhere, greeting the women and children from town and getting them quickly settled. It was as though the Sioux were happy to see them all and greeted them like old friends.

As they came to a particular teepee, Tanner reached out and scratched the outside of the flap. A moment later, a woman came out of the teepee carrying a small child in her arms. She smiled brightly at Tanner, and then to Bethany and Matilda.

"It is good to see you, Deputy. I was certain we would never get you here at camp," the woman said.

"Morning Sun, it is good to see you as well. Edward has been working hard back at the town and we are grateful for his support. He's convinced that he and the miners are fit enough to take care of the outlaws themselves," Tanner said with a chuckle. Morning Sun returned the gesture as she shook her head.

"That man could use a good fight. After all the pent-up anger he still has towards that white army, I am sure he will be of good use," Morning Sun said. "My new friends, welcome."

"Thank you," Bethany said, having realized she had been staring at the women. She spoke such good English that it was hard to see her as an Indian of the stories she had heard growing up.

"Come in and be settled. There is plenty of room for us all," Morning Sun said as she pulled back the hide flap of the teepee. Matilda took her trunk from Bethany and went right inside, and Bethany helped Tanner untie hers from his horse's saddle before stepping inside. She was surprised by the size of it and found a spot next to Matilda on the far side where there didn't seem to be many things. Several leather sacks hung from the teepee poles overhead, while there was a section of wicker baskets that Bethany could only assume held the personal belongings of the family.

"Well, I hate to leave you ladies, but I better get back down to the town," Tanner said as he stepped inside the teepee after Morning Sun. "But I know my friends here will take good care of you."

"I'll walk with you a ways," Bethany said as she thanked Morning Sun and promised to be right back.

"Take your time," Morning Sun said with a smile as she set her toddling child down. The baby squealed with excitement to see someone new.

Bethany stepped outside of the teepee with Tanner, looking around at the mix of people as many of the town's women and children were settled with various Indian families.

"I can't believe I'm standing in a real Indian camp," Bethany said, marveling at it all.

"I could say the same thing," Tanner said with a sigh. "Never thought I'd ever step foot up here."

"Thank you," Bethany said, remembering Tanner's anxiety around Indians. "This really means a lot to us."

"I wanted to make sure you and Matilda were taken care of, and I knew I had the spare time," Tanner said, looking at Bethany and offering her a smile. She went to him then and embraced him, not knowing when she would see him again. If the fighting was to begin soon, then Bethany wanted to spend a special moment with her future husband.

"Don't worry. Everything is going to work out fine," Tanner said, rubbing his hand over her back as he returned her embrace.

"Doesn't mean I'm still not going to worry," she said in a soft voice, trying hard to not let her emotions get the best of her. She wanted to be strong for Tanner when inside she feared for him and the men of Bear Creek who would remain in town and try to protect it.

"Well, you enjoy pretending to live like an Indian for a few days. The moment it is safe, I'll be back up here to bring you home myself." The idea that Bear Creek was now her home brought a sense of peace to her raging emotions. She allowed the embrace to continue on a few moments more before she let go of Tanner.

"Take care of yourself, Tanner. I'll be praying for you," Bethany said as she created some space between them.

"The same goes for you," Tanner said as he smiled at her before hoisting himself up onto the horse's saddle. They shared another tender look before he turned his horse around and slowly made his way back through all the teepees and the people all around. She stood there and watched him 'til he was out of sight. Then she went back into the teepee to make herself useful.

CHAPTER 24

There was a good group of men and Indians in the town hall that night. They had all gathered together to hear what the plan would be from the sheriff and the mayor. Tanner stood at the front next to Jacob and the mayor stood in what was normally Pastor Munster's spot when he was in town to give sermons. All eyes were on the mayor, and when it seemed everyone who was able had arrived, Mr. Franklin cleared his throat and gathered the attention of the room.

"Good evening, gentlemen. It pleases me to see you all here tonight. If I had to guess, I'd say there are at least a hundred of us between the folk of Bear Creek, and our friends from the Sioux Indian tribe," he said, a pleased grin upon his face as he surveyed the room. "I doubt any other town in Montana that has been devastated by this group of outlaws has been this prepared or had this many numbers on their side.

"Tonight, we will discuss the information we have on these outlaws that we are sure not even the marshal of

Montana knew about. We expect that the outlaws will either make their attack some time tonight, or in the early morning hours. That is why we had all the women, children, and unable men head to the Sioux camp where they have been reported to all be settled and are being taken care of by our Sioux friends.

"At one point today, the six sisters who had been discovered to be assisting the outlaws were released from jail. They have agreed to aid us in taking down these outlaws because they've been treated as slaves and prostitutes for over five years. They want their freedom as bad as we want to protect this town and our livelihood. Their correspondent came and got them today while we were all busy helping the women and children. But fear not! Three of Brown Bear's best trackers are on their trail and will report back to us soon with the location of the outlaws.

"Thanks to the Sioux, we will soon learn the whereabouts of the outlaws' camp, when they will be heading our way, and we'll have a better idea of their numbers. You are given the freedom to apprehend these outlaws anyway you see fit, but if they surrender, you're not to hurt them, but bind them. You all will be given cords fit for the job. The idea is to arrest as many as possible, not to murder them all. These men need to see that they are not above the law.

"Finally, I want you all to visit with one another and see what ammo and supplies can be shared. We want to make sure everyone has a weapon and enough metal cartridges to go around. Small groups of men will be put together and set at different parts of the town to keep an eye out for the incoming outlaws. It's going to be a long night, so make sure to look after one another and give everyone a turn to get some sleep."

Tanner listened intently for the next hour as the plan was hashed out. The Sioux would climb to the rooftops of all the buildings and perch there in order to shoot their long-distance arrows. Those on the ground would be responsible for spotting and stopping the Blackfoot Indians who had the job of lighting fire to the buildings. They weren't sure what Samantha had meant by mountain men but could only assume that they would be brute force fighters that would need to be stopped right away. As for the three brothers, they sure didn't know what to expect, but Jacob and Tanner would be hiding out at the bank to make the official arrest.

Right when everyone seemed to be ready to head out of the town hall, get something to eat, and get into position, one of the scouts that had been following the six sisters came running into the town hall and straight to the front to speak with Brown Bear.

"They are not far," he said in English for all to hear him. "South of town, around the bend of the mountains where the cliffs are too high to climb. They will need to come around to the main dirt road and right into town." Tanner thought about that path and hoped that the Jenkins' ranch would be spared as the outlaws made their way towards them.

"Do they look to be gathering to move?" Brown Bear asked.

"No, they look as if they are settling in for the night. It is quiet at camp, but the women are being watched over. If there is any sign that they have betrayed us, we will know," the Indian said.

"Very good, Dawn Runner. Return to your spot with your brothers and come running when they start to move our way.

You will be very important in this attack and must be prepared to sound the alarm," Brown Bear said, placing his hand on the Indian's shoulder. Tanner looked at the warrior, thinking they had to be about the same age. The Indian nodded his head before taking off back through the town hall as fast as the wind itself.

"This is good news," Jacob said to Brown Bear. "Now that we know their location, we know which direction to be facing as we look out into the night."

"Even so, all directions must be watched. The Blackfoot are good, stealthy Indians. We must not underestimate their ability to appear anywhere," Brown Bear said, his voice stern, that of a strong Indian chief. He was focused only on the mission at hand and would be a reliable fighter when things started to get heated.

"Alright, it's time to move out. Go fill those bellies and get to your assigned spots!" Jacob called over everyone in the town hall. Brown Bear likewise instructed his warriors in their native language to get into position and to remain like guardians, quick to defend.

Tanner was pretty sure he wasn't going to be able to eat anything that night, as he was so full of nerves. He wasn't sure quite what to expect even though a detailed plan had been put into place. They would wait in the darkness, listening to the sounds of the night, peering out into the distance around town. When the sound of a dove bird was heard, echoing throughout, that was the sign the Indian runner would make as he came to warn the town that the outlaws were on their way.

Tanner made his way across town and to the bank. As he stepped inside, he found a small lantern on the counter, its flame rather low, as Mr. Fritz stood there eating a corned beef sandwich. He waved at Tanner, signaling for him to come closer and join him.

"My wife made plenty of food before she went up to camp with her daughter and grandchildren. Please, eat or these outlaws will probably be able to smell us before they even make it to the front door," Mr. Fritz said as he chuckled. Tanner didn't want to be rude, so he took a bit of sandwich and started to eat. He only hoped that his nerves would stay calm enough for the food to settle and for him to remain alert at all times. Not soon after, Jacob joined them at the bank.

"Howdy there, fellas. Looks like a good old picnic happening at the bank," Jacob said, trying to use humor to cut the tension of the night. Tanner smiled, but he couldn't make himself chuckle like Mr. Fritz could.

"Join us for some fine cold sandwiches made from the finest corned beef you ever did have. My wife made it herself, so it's best not to call it anything else but the finest," Mr. Fritz quipped. Tanner smiled, thinking that was a reasonable statement. Mrs. Fritz had to learn a lot about cooking when she first came to Bear Creek with her daughter. Having been from a wealthy family, she'd never had to cook for herself. Most of the time she cooked well, and other times she still had a hard time.

"I bet all the women are having a great feast tonight," Jacob said. "Since they all know how to cook so well and take care of one another, I bet they are all comfy and fine."

"No doubt about it. Margret is such a social butterfly that I'm sure she's visited with every family to make sure they're alright. The Sioux have been such a blessing to this town that I have no worries about them all being up there," Mr. Fritz replied.

Tanner chewed his food and thought about Bethany. She had been exposed to so many new things in such a small amount of time that he truly wondered how she was doing. He had introduced her to a few of the families in Bear Creek, but would that be enough to help her feel comfortable in a new place? He just hoped that Matilda was making sure her friend was well cared for and would be comfortable enough to get some sleep that night. No doubt everyone would be worrying and wondering what would happen by morning. Tanner was a little worried himself. He knew that the biggest battle of his life was about to commence and it would take every able person in Bear Creek to make it a successful one.

After the food was eaten and everyone's basic needs were taken care of, they decided that it would be Mr. Fritz who would try to get some sleep first. Tanner wasn't sure if he would be able to sleep at all, but knew it would be important to remain sharp and alert when it was his turn to be lookout. As Mr. Fritz went to the back room to lie down on the cot that was there, Jacob extinguished the lantern, causing the bank to be covered in darkness. With their eyes straining to see the door, Tanner and Jacob began to wait for the fight to begin.

CHAPTER 25

Bethany sat around a central fire, which had been built up to shed plenty of light on the number of women and a few men that were gathered to eat dinner. She was sitting on a log with Matilda on one side of her and Morning Sun on the other. She was thankful to have made a quick Indian friend who could explain everything to her and Matilda. There was sure a lot to learn about the Indian way of life. And she reckoned that it was all a good distraction from the danger that was happening below in the town.

"The women there are all preparing the meal for this evening. It is a soft bread mixed with deer meat and root vegetables. Similar to your shepherd's pie. When the food is ready for everyone, it will be divided onto clay plates and passed around to everyone gathered tonight. The hands are used to eat," Morning Sun explained. She smiled as she saw Bethany and Matilda's reaction to eating with their hands, but neither one of the ladies would complain when the food smelled so delicious.

"It seems as though all the Indian women work together compared to white families who often just feed their own immediate family members," Bethany reasoned.

"That is a good comparison. Yes, the women are responsible for preparing the meals and cleaning the animals that the men hunt for in the mornings. We do many things for the tribe, including making clothing and making sure things stay clean," Morning Sun explained.

"It sounds like a lot of hard work," Matilda said.

"Not when everyone works together," Morning Sun pointed out. "If one woman is done with her work for the day, she will go to another teepee and help with the work. I am a mother of a young child. Many older women come to help me."

"This is a lovely community. The Indian women have been quick to help us strangers," Bethany said softly.

"It is a good way to show the people of Bear Creek that the Sioux are a peaceful people. And the people of Bear Creek did help us when the white army came last year to try to move us off this land. It is only natural that we help in return when another army comes to threaten the people of the town," Morning Sun explained.

"That is a nice way of looking at things. I was able to meet the woman who will be marrying the Indian chief. She is not an Indian," Bethany pointed out. Morning Sun chuckled and nodded.

"Yes, she was not born an Indian. But she might as well be one," Morning Sun said. "She has the heart of an Indian woman and will make a good partner for Brown Bear. She does not speak often, so I know those two will not be able to argue very loudly." This made Bethany laugh as she reasoned that was a good thing. "And I am married to a man who is half-Indian. My parents at first would not accept him and give him permission for us to marry. But he proved himself to be very worthy. I am so happy that we are married now."

"I am happy for you," Bethany said, seeing how blissful Morning Sun looked as she talked about married life. She was holding a sleeping child in her arms and yet looked happy and content to be a mother.

"You will soon be marrying Tanner Williams, right?" Morning Sun asked, a knowing smile on her face.

"Yes, that is true. Once all this trouble is behind us," Bethany agreed. "And Matilda here is going to open a laundry business." She didn't want her best friend to feel left out of the conversation and quickly included her.

"It is very interesting to think of a woman who will be owning a business in town," Morning Sun commented. "I hope you will have lots of success, and no troublemakers from the men." They all laughed at that comment and agreed that it might stir up some bad opinions, but that Matilda would not let that stop her from being a big success.

When the food was finally finished, Bethany watched as it was portioned out on the plates, and everyone passed down a plate around the fire until everyone had something to eat. Children were coaxed into sitting on their mothers' feet to sit still and eat their dinner. Thankfully, most of the children had been excited about the idea of staying with Indians, as though it was all a big adventure. Despite the dangers that loomed over the town, Bethany could at least see that everyone was staying in high spirits and making sure there was enough food for everyone. Even the Indian maidens helped the mothers who had many children. There were more than enough helping hands to ensure everyone had enough to eat, and the children remained safe.

There was a lot of chattering and laughter around the central fire that night. The few warriors that had been tasked to watch over the women circled around, always keeping an eye on the tree line in case trouble made its way to the camp. Matilda and Bethany talked more about the business she wanted to open in town, and after a while, Bethany felt as though she was comfortable enough to fall asleep that night. She felt safe amongst all the women and children and hoped by morning there would be good news from Tanner that the troublesome outlaws had been taken care of.

When all the food had been eaten, the plates were passed back around the central fire to be collected and washed. Bethany thought it best to make herself useful, so she helped the Indian maidens in washing the dishes. It also gave her the opportunity to wash up her hands and arms so she would be ready for sleep that night. As the task was finishing up, Bethany returned to Morning Sun as she and Matilda followed the Indian woman back to her teepee.

Bethany never thought she would ever sleep in an Indian teepee. Though she knew Morning Sun was married to a white man who owned and managed the mines, she still felt as though she was living a dream. Morning Sun showed them how to sleep on the pelts that were used to soften the ground. Furs were then pulled up over them to keep them warm during the cool nights. Bethany and Matilda didn't even bother changing into nightgowns. They simply undressed to their chemises and tried to get as comfortable as possible on their spot in the teepee.

Facing each other, Bethany whispered to Matilda, "Can you believe we're sleeping in a teepee?"

Matilda smiled as she shrugged her shoulders. "Beats being stuck in Tennessee, doing the same things over and over again for absolutely nothing. At least here we are living an adventurous life and experiencing things people have never talked about before."

"I certainly agree with that thought," Bethany replied, stifling a yawn as she did so. "These furs are actually really comfortable to sleep with."

"A lot better than the cushions on the train," Matilda added. "Though I do miss a proper bed."

"I like to think that we will be able to live a normal life soon," Bethany said. "I'm excited to marry Tanner and to learn what my day-to-day life will be."

"You are lucky that Tanner turned out to be such a nice guy. You're probably the luckiest woman in the world," Matilda said. Bethany could hear her sigh in the darkness of the teepee.

"You will marry one day, too. There are many single men in Bear Creek, and you never know. You could fall madly in love with one of them," Bethany said, a smile coming to her face as she tried to imagine Matilda's perfect husband.

"Well, if I have a successful washing business, I suppose I won't need a husband," Matilda reasoned.

"But how will you have a family without a husband?"

"I will become so wealthy that I'll just adopt a bunch of children," Matilda said with a chuckle.

"As nice an idea as that is, I'm sure you'd like to be in love, too."

"I will love all my adopted children so much that there would be no more love for a husband." The women chuckled at the thought and eventually quieted down. It would be rude to keep Morning Sun and her child up all night with their random chattering.

Bethany rolled onto her back and looked up at the top of the teepee where the fire smoke escaped. She could see stars in the sky and couldn't help but wonder what Tanner was doing that very moment.

As she started to drift off to sleep, she thought of a silent prayer in her mind. She prayed that the people of Bear Creek would be protected, that the Sioux people would be blessed for their help to the town's people, and that one day Matilda would meet a man with whom she could fall in love.

CHAPTER 26

Tanner felt someone shake his shoulder gently, rousing him back to life after falling asleep sometime in the early morning. It had finally come his time to get some rest, but he felt it had just been a moment ago when he'd fallen asleep. He blinked his eyes a few times and noticed that Jacob was kneeling by his side, waking him. The second thing he noticed was the dim morning sun barely peeking over the horizon to cast a faint light all around.

"It's go time," Jacob whispered, helping Tanner to his feet. Tanner then noticed the faint sound of a dove as though it was swooping through town and heading off in the other direction. Tanner grabbed for his revolver at his side, pulling it from the leather holster and checking to make sure each of the eight chambers had a bullet in it. He then followed Jacob to the front of the bank where they all got perched behind the counter.

The hardest part about hiding out in the bank to capture the three brothers was having to sit and listen to the chaos that soon seemed to ensue all around them. First they heard the war cry of the Sioux Indians, followed by cries of pain and shouting as their arrows were loosed and buried into their targets. Someone yelled "fire" and Tanner desperately wanted to go and help put it out. All the buildings were so close in town that one fire would surely lead to another and another. Gun fire started to ring out next into the early morning hour, the mixture of fighting and screams soon filling the air.

"Those bitches must have lied to us," came a voice as someone entered the bank. "There are plenty of townspeople fighting back. And it's like they have a whole army of savages with them."

"Doesn't matter, Eddy. Let's get this money and get out of here. We can start all over in another state and continue our mission of purification," said another.

As three sets of footsteps made their way towards the counter, Jacob gave the signal to the other men. At once in one swift movement, the sheriff, the deputy, and the banker stood together and focused their weapons on the three men that had stepped into the bank. Thankfully, these men didn't have a weapon drawn and were completely caught off guard. They all quickly raised their hands, shocked to discover that it had all been a trap.

"Alright, boys. On your knees," Jacob said as he slowly stepped out from behind the counter. Tanner followed, keeping his eyes and gun focused on the middle man while Mr. Fritz and Jacob focused their weapons on the other two. Mr. Fritz was wielding a shotgun that would probably take out all three based on how close he was to them.

As the three men knelt down, the one on the end closest to Jacob reached for his gun so swiftly, that all Tanner could think was to get Jacob out of the way. He had a wife and child, after all, and he couldn't bear telling Mrs. Benning her husband had died. Three things happened at the same time. Tanner jumped and knocked Jacob out of the way the same moment the outlaw fired his gun and Mr. Fritz fired his shotgun. Five bodies hit the ground at the same time. The three outlaws had taken the full brunt of Mr. Fritz's shotgun. Tanner had landed on top of Jacob and quickly rolled off as he raised his revolver and prepared to fire. But it didn't look like the outlaws were going to get up any time soon. A strange pain entered Tanner's body as he realized that the three brothers were probably dead, and he reached down and pressed the wet spot that had started to form on his stomach.

Tanner rested his head on the floorboards of the bank as he pressed his palm into the bullet wound in his side. He understood what he'd done, how he'd saved Jacob's life at the cost of his own. And as he lay there, unable to really hear anything that was going on around him, he accepted his fate. He would die from saving his best friend's life. He wouldn't be able to marry Bethany after all, and prayed she would one day find love again. Tanner was content with having met a woman he wanted to marry, and with ensuring that this town would still have its amazing sheriff. As Tanner closed his eyes, he was at peace.

BETHANY WOKE QUICKLY to the sound of a great commotion

outside. She lifted her head, propping herself up on her elbow as her body cramped. She had a terrible pain in her side from where she'd slept funny. She rubbed it with her free hand as she tried to make sense of what the noise was. As Matilda was awoken as well, the women quickly stood and threw on their gowns so at least they were decent when they stepped out of the teepee and faced where all the noise was coming from.

In the distance, near the central fire, she could see that Brown Bear had returned. He was a tall Indian and easy to see over crowds. Matilda and Bethany took off through camp, joining others who had been woken by the noise of the warriors returning to camp. Bethany was anxious to know what had happened, along with all the other people currently at camp.

"The battle has been won!" yelled Brown Bear over the crowd of mostly women gathered around the Indian chief. He raised his arms over his head, a look of triumph on his face. A loud cheer rose up in the air then as everyone cried out in joy. Women hugged their children closely, looks of relief all around. Brown Bear's future bride pushed through the crowd and quickly embraced Brown Bear. And he in turn swung her around as he laughed for joy.

Bethany looked around to see if Tanner had joined the Indians that had returned to camp. All she saw was a stream of Indian warriors who were returning to their homes, dirty and bloody. The battle might have been won, but at what cost? She saw a string of Indians with messy black hair and dirty clothes that were being led by a Sioux warrior. Their wrists were all tied together, and they were connected to one long rope. They looked around at the cheering tribe, a mixture of Sioux and white people. And the scene before them seemed to trouble them deeply.

"I want to return to town to learn what has happened," Bethany said as she rubbed her sore side. "I need to know that Tanner is alright."

"Do you think that is a wise idea?" Matilda asked. "Did Tanner not promise you that he would come up to camp?"

"Yes, I know what he said. But I am anxious to see him," Bethany admitted.

"Let us go down after we have washed up and eaten some breakfast. We will learn more about what happened from the Indians and see if it is even safe to return back to town. It may be a mess right now, and not something that women and children should witness," Matilda explained. Bethany didn't like the idea of having to wait much longer but decided that her friend was more than likely correct.

Bethany and Matilda made their way through the crowd and back to the teepee of Morning Sun. Inside, they shared the news with their host, and together the three women prepared a simple breakfast of what Bethany would describe as porridge with some fresh berries that Morning Sun had. Bethany would agree it was a decent breakfast, but she couldn't get rid of the gut feeling in her stomach that she desperately wanted to see Tanner for herself and make sure he was alright.

When the breakfast was finished, Matilda helped Morning Sun take the dishes to be washed while Bethany tended to the little child. She tried to focus on entertaining the toddler instead of her worries. She felt a sense of relief knowing that the Sioux and the townspeople had been successful in apprehending the outlaws, but how was the town? What about the people? And more importantly, how was Tanner doing?

When the teepee flap shifted again, Bethany looked up, expecting to see Morning Sun and Matilda. But instead, she was faced with a very exhausted man who looked quite dirty.

"You are not my Morning Sun, yet you are here with our child," Edward said with a small grin. He came and sat down heavily, gesturing towards the child. In turn, Flying Jay crawled over to him and started babbling incoherent words.

"Morning Sun and my friend Matilda went to the stream to wash the breakfast dishes. My name is Bethany Duncan. I'm here in Bear Creek to be Tanner Williams' wife," Bethany explained. Edward seemed to perk up at the mention of Tanner, and his brown eyes went dark. It was then she could notice the half Indian in him.

"Tanner's in the clinic right now, being operated on by Dr. Roberts," Edward said in a grave voice. Bethany felt like she'd been punched in the gut as all the air left her lungs and she became very still.

"What happened?" she asked, her voice barely a whisper. She felt her head start to spin, but she refused to faint.

"He got shot in the gut saving the sheriff," Edward said. "It was a brutal fight, the likes of which I have never seen before. There were so many of them that at first it was overwhelming. But everyone stuck to the plan and either ended their lives or were able to convince them to surrender. The three behind the whole thing died in the battle."

"That all sounds so gruesome," she reasoned. "How is Tanner doing?"

"Won't know 'til the doc patches him back up. I would

suggest you head down to the town to check on him, but it's not a place for women to be right now. Most of the inn caught fire, and there is a lot of clean up to be done, if you know what I mean," Edward said. "You and your friend are more than welcome to stay with us 'til things get situated."

"Would you take me down to see Tanner?" she asked, knowing she was asking too much from the exhausted man.

"I sure will," he replied with a smile. "Just let me get cleaned and catch a few hours of sleep. But I promise I'll take you down on horseback so it will be a fast trip and you can see Tanner today."

"Thank you," Bethany said, feeling a bit relieved. She then gathered the babbling child in her arms and went outside to give Edward the privacy he needed to get cleaned up and rest. She was playing outside with the child when Matilda and Morning Sun returned.

"Edward is inside, resting," Bethany told Morning Sun as she approached. "I was out here to let him sleep."

"The man can sleep through anything. You will not wake him when he is asleep," Morning Sun replied. "I will take this little troublemaker and join the big troublemaker. You two make yourselves at home." The woman went inside with the small child, carrying the clean dishes in a basket inside the teepee. Bethany faced Matilda, tears in her eyes.

"Edward told me it was a gruesome battle and that Tanner was shot saving the sheriff. Supposedly Dr. Roberts is working on him now," Bethany said in a weak voice. She didn't want to start sobbing when she didn't know how he really was. But just the thought of him hurt and perhaps soon to pass away caused her such pain, that it frightened her at first to feel this way. It was proof of how much she had come to care for Tanner in a short amount of time.

"There, there. Everything will be fine," Matilda said as she embraced Bethany. "The outlaws are done for, and that is what is most important. Tanner will need some time to heal, and then the two of you will be getting married and having all sorts of babies." Bethany couldn't help but chuckle through her tears at the way her friend spoke. She was so thankful to have Matilda in her life.

"Edward said he'd give me a ride to the town later after he's rested," Bethany explained after she had calmed down. "What do you think we should do 'til then?"

"There is a whole tribe of people, and those from the town who could probably use some help," Matilda said as she looked around. "Perhaps if we offered up some help we can not only learn more about what happened, but I can also talk to other women about my laundry business."

Matilda had a bright smile on her face, and Bethany couldn't resist going along with the plan in order to help her friend. Bethany thought that perhaps if they spent some time serving others, she would panic less about what condition Tanner was currently in. But it seemed that no matter how hard she worked, she couldn't stop worrying.

CHAPTER 27

Tanner felt a burning sensation in his side but felt too tired to do anything about it. The pain from the bullet hole washed over his body like waves of fire. Sometimes the pain would die down, and other times it would flare up. And all the while, he was left to the mercy of this pain because he couldn't raise himself enough to even see what was going on. All he could do was feel the pain and pray that it would be over soon.

He brought to his mind the image of Bethany. First, he saw the picture Bethany had sent to him in her first letter. Tanner thought of every detail of the picture just so his mind had something else to focus on besides the pain. He thought of Bethany when he had first seen her in person. He remembered her radiant blonde hair and her happy personality even though she was clearly exhausted. Tanner liked how happy she seemed to be even though she'd just traveled a really long distance to come to a remote town. But she had taken all the new experiences like one giant adventure.

Tanner thought about seeing Bethany right before he went back down to the town from the Indian camp. He brought to his mind the feeling of her in his arms as he held her tight, the smell of her hair as she pressed her cheek against his. The sound of her voice as she whispered to him. It was all swirling in his mind as he tried as hard as he could to block out the pain. But eventually the pain won, and he fell into a pit of darkness where he felt nothing at all.

The next thing Tanner remembered was blinking his eyes open. When his vision focused, he noticed a ceiling made of wooden boards. A lantern was hanging from a hook in the ceiling, casting just enough light into the space that he could see a bit. Slowly, Tanner turned his head ever so slightly as his skin sweated from the heat he was still experiencing. He was in a lot of pain but needed to be able to see where he was.

Sitting at his side like a statue was Bethany. He focused on her and saw how she was looking down at his hand. He used all his strength to twitch his hand, causing her to stir. And then, when her eyes met his, he couldn't help but smile as her face lit up with excitement.

"Tanner, you're awake," she exclaimed. He tried to nod his head, but even that hurt. "Don't move. Let me get Dr. Roberts," she said, rising from the chair and disappearing.

Tanner tried to turn his head again and see where she'd run off to, but it was a very tiring and hard thing to do. He could see now that he was in the clinic, lying on a cot. He listened and heard the groans from other men, thinking that the clinic must be pretty full after the fight they had all experienced. He desperately wanted to know what the outcome had been and how everyone else was doing.

"Hey there, Deputy," Dr. Roberts said in a soft voice as he came closer. He sat down in the chair that Bethany had been occupying a moment ago and quickly pulled out his stethoscope. He pressed it to Tanner's bare chest. It was only then that Tanner realized that all he was wearing was the wool blanket that had been tucked around him. He wasn't sure where all his clothes had gone but he was sure there was a reason for all of that.

"How are you feeling?" Dr. Roberts asked. "Seems like you still have that fever." Tanner licked his lips to say something but felt so tired.

"Blink your eyes if you're in pain?" Dr. Roberts said then as he leaned closer. Tanner blinked his eyes three times, hoping the doctor would get the message.

"Alright, Tanner. I'll give you some more pain meds, but when you wake up next you're going to have to eat and drink something before I gave you anymore," he said. Tanner tried to nod his head, but felt the pain quickly rising up once more. He parted his lips for the bitter medicine the doctor fed him on a spoon, and it wasn't long before it started to take effect and he could relax once more.

Bethany switched spots with the doctor when someone else came to call on him. He smiled up at Bethany, thinking how pretty she looked. He was so glad that she was there by his side, and that he could confirm that she was alright. And, if she was in town, that must have meant something good had happened. She reached for his hand and grasped it, and with most of the pain gone, he was able to squeeze her hand back. Soon after, he fell deeply asleep once more.

SEEING Tanner's pale body was a torment to Bethany. The fact that he'd woken for a small time meant that he would pull through after having a bullet hole in his gut and being sewn back together. It gave Bethany hope that Tanner would pull through and recover in a few weeks. With so much damage having been caused in town, it was good to know that both the sheriff and the deputy would be around to tell this tale one day.

When Tanner was resting once more, Bethany let go of his hand and stood from the chair she'd been occupying for hours. She needed to stretch her legs and get something to eat before she started to feel unwell herself. But as she stepped out of the clinic and looked around at the destruction, she wasn't really sure where she would be able to eat that night and would no doubt have to make it back to camp just to eat.

Across the street from the clinic was a pile of burnt rubble that used to be the inn. It was the only building that had burned down, but since it was such an important part of the town, and the place where most people had their meals, it was a huge loss. The cries of Mrs. Tibet had been heard upon coming down from the camp to view her and her husband's life's work. They had raised a family in that inn and had served hundreds of people over the years. Now, it was a smoldering pile of lumber that couldn't even be touched 'til the last of the smoke had stopped.

In the setting sun, Bethany could make out red patches of earth in the road where someone had been killed. She tried not to look at these marks and instead took deep breaths as she watched all the people walking about up and down the town. Many had somber looks upon their faces. She pressed her back up against the clinic wall, trying to stay out of the way. By the time Edward had brought her to town, thankfully all those that had lost their lives had been buried, and the outlaws that had surrendered were now in a jail cell. A telegram had been sent to the Montana marshal, declaring that the outlaws had been taken care of, and that the territory was now safe from their tyranny.

Bethany knew that she should be happy that the majority of the town still stood, and that not a single Sioux or townsperson had lost their lives. All the casualties from the battle had been from the outlaws. And after all the destruction that had taken place the last few months by these evil men, it was a fitting end for most of them. Bethany was sure the rest of them that had survived the battle and were now sitting in a jail cell would hang for their crimes once handed over to the marshal.

"How is Tanner doing?" Edward asked as he made his way back to the clinic, having done his best to help out now that he'd gotten some rest.

"He woke for a bit," Bethany explained. "Dr. Roberts gave him some more medicine to take away his pain and help him sleep."

"That has to be a good thing if he woke up for a bit. I bet by morning he'll be back to normal," Edward said encouragingly. "We should probably head back up to camp before it gets dark. I know the way, but the forest at night can be pretty spooky for a woman. Plus, dinner will be served soon, and I don't know about you, but I could eat a horse." Bethany chuckled, knowing the man was only trying to help her smile. There was so much dismay and death around them that perhaps the best thing to do was look for whatever positive was left for the day. And that would be a decent meal.

Bethany walked with Edward towards where his Indian pony had been left in the corral at the livery stables. As they were crossing the road, Mr. Fritz hurried towards them, waving a piece of paper in his hands.

"Miss Duncan. I never did give you the deposit certificate," Mr. Fritz said. "I wanted you to be reassured that your money is safe at the bank."

"Thank you, Mr. Fritz," Bethany said as she took the piece of paper. "How are you doing?"

"I'm faring just fine. Those evil men have been laid to rest, and I know the devil is making them pay for their many crimes," Mr. Fritz said with confidence. "I'll be collecting my horse soon and heading up to camp to reassure Mrs. Fritz all is well."

"We are headed that way as well," Edward said. "Care to join us?"

"That would be nice, so I don't have to ride alone," Mr. Fritz replied.

Bethany folded the piece of paper and stuck it into the pocket of her apron. She walked with the gentlemen to the livery stables where the horses were collected. Bethany sat on the Indian pony with her legs dangling over the sides. She had to hold on to Edward's shoulders to maintain her balance as the pony made quick work of returning to the camp. It was much faster than walking the distance, but she thought she would much prefer riding her own horse with a proper saddle and reins to control. This pony seemed to know just where to go and what to do, so it was up to her and Edward to just hold on.

The smell of cooked food filled the area as they got closer to camp. The sun had almost set, and she was glad they were able to make it back before it became too dark. She slid off the back of the Indian pony as they broke through the tree line and Edward pulled the animal to a stop.

"Thank you, Edward. I will let the others know we have returned," Bethany said before heading towards the central fire. It seemed like a good group had gathered that night. The Indians seemed to be celebrating the victory, while many of the town's folk were more somber. After all, the inn had been lost in the fire. And there were seven farms that had been burned down to the ground.

"Ah, there you are," Matilda said as Bethany sat down on a log next to her.

"We just got back," Bethany explained, looking to both Matilda and Morning Sun.

"How is Tanner doing?" Morning Sun asked.

"He was able to wake for a short time. So that was a good sign. I will try to go see him in the morning," Bethany explained.

"How does the town look?" Matilda asked.

"Rough," Bethany admitted. "The inn was burnt to the ground, and it was horrible to hear Mrs. Tibet cry so. There is a lot of evidence that a battle took place around town, so I agree that it isn't a place for women and children to be until it can all be cleaned up."

"White Raven, our medicine man, said he will pray for rains tonight so it can wash the earth of this evil," Morning Sun explained. Bethany wasn't sure what a medicine man was, but the idea of it raining and washing the land certainly sounded like a good idea.

Edward soon joined their little group around the central fire just in time for the food to start being passed around the circle of people. The chatter quieted down while everyone ate. It was deer meat stew once more. It was thick enough that it was easy to eat with the fry bread and just using the fingers to eat. Bethany was thankful for the food, and for a place to sleep that night. Until she was married, she would certainly need to find a good place to sleep because the inn was no more.

When Bethany was done eating and had done a decent job at cleaning her fingers, she pulled out the certificate Mr. Fritz had given her and looked down at the number printed on it. She hadn't realized she had been carrying so much money with her and really thought this would be a good amount for what she wanted to do. Once she went into town the next day, she would put this exciting plan into play and hopefully get Bear Creek back to normal even sooner.

CHAPTER 28

"Are you sure this is what you want to do?" Tanner asked as he sat up on the cot. By the next afternoon, he'd regained at least enough strength to where he could sit up instead of lying down all the time.

"Yes, I absolutely want to help as much as I can. I don't think we need all this money right now, and could certainly invest it back in the town," Bethany said. "And I can always go and work for Matilda. I know she would pay me well."

"With this amount of money, we could live easy lives and even hire people to do things for us, like clean and cook," Tanner reasoned.

"Yes, that is true. But take it from someone who lived an entire life having people do things for her. There is a certain amount of pride I get for doing things for myself. I think we would become bored in life if it was easy all the time," Bethany replied. The sound of thunder was heard overhead then, and Tanner waited for the sound to pass before he spoke again. It had been raining all night and morning, yet Bethany had still come to visit him at the clinic, practically soaked through.

"It's your money, so ultimately it's your decision."

"But you will soon be my husband. Therefore, it is our decision," Bethany said with a smile. Tanner reached over and took her hand, squeezing it. It felt good to know that Bethany already saw him as her husband and was including him in this big choice.

"I think what you are willing to do for the Tibets and the farmers is a great thing. You should talk it over with Mr. Franklin and Jacob. Those two could really give you a hand," Tanner said.

"I think my ears are burning," the sheriff said as he came down the row of cots and came to stand at the foot of Tanner's cot.

"Speak of the devil and he shall appear," Tanner quipped.

"How's my hero feeling?" Jacob asked, a grin on his face.

"Like I got shot with a bullet for no good reason," Tanner said, trying hard not to laugh. His stomach was mighty sore, and his entire side still hurt pretty badly.

"Well, you better rest up and heal fast so you can marry this fine lady," Jacob said. "She won't wait on you forever." Tanner rolled his eyes at that comment while Bethany laughed. It was such a pleasing sound that Tanner hoped he would be able to make her laugh always.

"Bethany here has an idea for helping out the Tibets and the other farmers that lost their properties to fire," Tanner said to Jacob.

"Oh, is that right?" Jacob asked, giving the young lady his attention.

"I have roughly three thousand dollars. I would like to purchase the lumber and labor needed to rebuild the inn, and the most important buildings the farmers will need. If there is enough money, I would like to also purchase supplies and other things the inn might need, like furniture," Bethany explained. Tanner tried really hard not to laugh as he watched Jacob's eyes grow large with surprise.

"You… you want to…you have how much money?" Jacob stammered.

"What? Do you think it won't be enough?" Bethany asked, looking between Tanner and Jacob with a look of confusion.

"Darling, it's going to be more than enough. I'm certain with everyone willing to pitch in, you'll even have extra money to do with as you please," Tanner said. "Especially since you haven't seen my small home yet."

"Smaller homes are easier to clean," Bethany said with a smile.

"My goodness, Tanner. You sure got yourself a fine young lady. I can't think of a kinder person besides my own Rosa," Jacob said, tears in his eyes.

"You going to make it, Sheriff?" Tanner asked, smiling brightly.

"Yeah, yeah. Just going to need a moment," Jacob said as he took a deep breath. "I'd be willing to walk you over to speak to the mayor about your idea. The Tibets have been staying with him at his house outside of town anyway."

"Alright, I'd like that," Bethany said. "You going to be alright without me for a bit?"

"Yes, I'll be just fine. Dr. Roberts has been keeping his eye on me," Tanner reassured. He squeezed her hand one more time before letting go. She leaned over and kissed him on the cheek before following Jacob out of the clinic. He was sure proud of the woman he'd be able to marry soon. Now all he had to do was feel well enough to stand up for the ceremony.

Bethany hurried over to the town hall with the sheriff as the rain continued to pour. It had stopped all the progress in town, but at least the ground showed no more evidence of a battle and the inn was no longer smoldering. Jacob held the door open for her as they hurried inside the town hall. She was in such a hurry that she almost ran into the towering figure of the Sioux chief.

"Do excuse me," Bethany said as she moved out of his way. She lowered her eyes, not wanting to offend him.

"No worry," Brown Bear replied, a kind smile on his face. "Hello there, Jacob Benning."

"Chief," Jacob replied.

"What brings you two in?" Mr. Franklin asked, appearing to have just finished up with a meeting with Brown Bear when Bethany and Jacob came running in from the rain.

"Mr. Mayor, I'd like to talk about using some of my own money to fund the rebuilding of the inn and other farming buildings that were lost in the attacks," Bethany explained. "I hear that the Tibets are staying with you during this time."

"Yes, they are," Mr. Franklin replied, his eyes shifting between Bethany and the sheriff as though to question if

Bethany was actually being serious. "You really have the money to do that?"

"I won't go into detail on how I acquired the money, but I do have a certificate from Mr. Fritz detailing that I have made a large deposit to the bank. I've been reassured that I have enough to fund the rebuilding," Bethany said.

"Is she serious, Jacob?" the mayor asked, surprised.

"Completely, Mr. Franklin. Miss Duncan here really does just want to help," Jacob said, a big grin on his face.

"My goodness, what a miracle. The inn is such a big part of Bear Creek that everyone would be really pleased to know it could be rebuilt sooner rather than later," the mayor said, the smile on his face growing as he talked.

"Trees will need to be cut and cured for the lumber needed to rebuild," Brown Bear said. "Perhaps this is the time that Bear Creek needs a lumber mill, as you have talked about." He was addressing the mayor then, and Bethany was curious about what else Bear Creek was in need of and just how far her money could go.

"This could be the business venture you've been looking for, Brown Bear. It will be more substantial than just a dozen Indian braves working in the mines for Mr. James. Bear Creek is in need of a lot of lumber to rebuild everything," Mr. Franklin said as he spoke to the Indian chief.

"Then I think this is fortunate timing," Brown Bear said as he focused his attention back on Bethany, smiling kindly at her. "Perhaps you and I can talk more about these ideas. My people need security for the future. By investing in Bear Creek, we have an easier time remaining on our lands and upholding our traditions and beliefs."

"I'm just willing to help where I can," Bethany admitted. "I don't have any special skills. But I do have a lot of money that could go towards a good cause."

For the next hour or so, Bethany sat down with the three gentlemen and talked about all sorts of ideas for Bear Creek. The lumber mill would give Bear Creek the opportunity to have local lumber. And, since the forest on the mountains was plentiful, there would be a good source of trees that could be processed, and once ready, could be used to rebuild many things that had been burned down. With every passing minute, Bethany felt sure she had made the right decision to offer up her resources for this big endeavor. She wasn't only going to help the inn be rebuilt. Bethany had the chance to help improve Bear Creek and make it into an even bigger town.

"And let's not forget what Tanner suggested. He thought it would be nice to have a rodeo right here in Bear Creek. It would bring people from all over. And if the inn was big enough, it could accommodate more people who'd want to travel to Bear Creek for different things. Heck, people would start coming to Bear Creek for lumber from neighboring towns instead of all the way north to Great Falls," Jacob said. Bethany liked the idea of a rodeo and to put into action something that Tanner had thought of.

By the time the meeting was over, it seemed they all had an idea of what the next steps would be. Bethany would need to speak to Mr. Fritz about allowing the Mayor to have access to her money so things could be purchased. She didn't know if there would be much left over from what she'd stolen from her father once all was said and done, but the idea of working with Matilda with her laundry business certainly made her think that she would never be without and would have a type of job she could be proud of. And she would be able to see her best friend every day as well.

The rain seemed to have finally stopped by the time the town hall was emptied. Bethany and Matilda had been offered Sandy Roberts' old room above the clinic. So Bethany made her way back over in that direction, wanting to help with dinner if she could. As she entered the clinic, she found Tanner resting again, having lain back down on the cot to get some sleep. She stood there a moment watching him, thinking how excited she was to tell him the good news in the morning.

Looking back on it all, Bethany knew that coming out to Bear Creek had been the right decision. She was happy with what she'd been able to accomplish so far, even though the life she was now living was nowhere close to the one she'd been born into. But she was no longer afraid of her future, and that is what impressed her the most. She would soon be marrying Tanner—as soon as he felt better—and that meant the world to her. She knew Tanner was a great man, and her heart started to fall deeply in love with the sleeping deputy.

CHAPTER 29

After another week and a half of resting in the clinic, Tanner finally felt ready to get up and moving. Bethany was at his side the entire time, his arm resting over her shoulders as they slowly walked together. Tanner felt weak all over even though he'd been resting most of the time. He still had a long road of recovery ahead of him, but with Bethany by his side, he felt as though he could accomplish anything.

The town seemed to almost be back to normal considering what they had faced. The farmers who had lost barns and houses were currently bunking down with other farmers and ranchers. The Jenkins' had taken in the Peters family, hiring the three men as cattle hands until the next planting season when they could get their farm back up and running. Similar situations had happened all over the outskirts of Bear Creek as families did their best to help one another.

The news of what Bethany was willing to do for the town

spread like wildfire and was the good news the people needed. The Tibets had been so overjoyed to hear that the inn would be rebuilt that they cried for joy and wouldn't let Bethany out of their embrace for a very long time. Even though they were staying with the mayor a little ways out of town to the south, they came into town every day to help out where they could and even continued to cook meals in the homes in town.

Matilda used the money she had earned so far to rent one of the vacant shops in town to start her laundering business. When Bethany wasn't helping Tanner get some exercise, she was with Matilda doing laundry. Matilda had explained over dinner one night with the Roberts that she wanted to get a horse and buggy so she could drive around to the different ranches and farms and offer to do their laundry and return it the next day. Tanner thought it was such a brilliant idea that he was certain she and Bethany would be a huge success.

More than anything, Tanner was excited to marry Bethany. He was determined to regain strength in his legs so he could stand at the front of the town hall and have Pastor Munster marry the two of them. He'd already written to the pastor, asking him to do the service the next time he was in town. And Mr. Fritz was helping him get two silver rings for the ceremony. It seemed that there was nothing else to be done before the wedding besides for him to start feeling better.

"You seem deep in thought today," Bethany said as she helped Tanner walk down the boardwalk towards Fry's so Bethany could get some more flour. She was going to help Mrs. Roberts make a cobbler pie that was supposed to rival even Mrs. Fritz's. Mrs. Roberts said she knew a recipe her mother had taught her that she wanted to try and see if it could possibly be any better, and perhaps cheer a few people up.

"Just thinking about everything that has happened, and how excited I am to finally get to marry you," Tanner admitted, smiling as he hobbled along with Bethany's support.

"Well, first you need to be able to hold yourself up on your own before we go tying the knot. So you just focus on getting better and all the other details will figure themselves out," Bethany said as they started to cross the street. They had just made it to the other side when they noticed a wagon coming into town from the south. Bethany helped Tanner down onto the wooden bench outside of the general goods store and they both saw the six sisters being driven into town on a wagon that was being manned by the sheriff himself.

"Howdy there," Jacob said as he waved to Tanner and Bethany. "Look at this bunch of fine young ladies I just found." Tanner could hardly believe it. The Indian scouts had lost track of the women when the fighting began, and to see them appear once more made Tanner feel relieved that they were actually still alive.

"Samantha!" Tanner called as he raised his hand and waved. The woman looked towards the sound of her name being called and waved back at Tanner. As Jacob pulled the two Clydesdales to a stop in front of the store, he wedged the brake pole into the front wheel before hopping down from the driver's seat and helping the young ladies down from the back of the wagon. They looked a little rough and a bit malnourished. But nothing that couldn't be remedied.

"Miss Duncan, may I introduce you to the latest additions to Bear Creek. These women are responsible for giving this town the fighting chance we needed in the battle against the outlaws. I'm very proud of them and think it's time we pay them back for everything they've done for us," Jacob said in a loud voice as though he was talking to a crowd instead of just Bethany. Tanner watched as Mr. Fry came out of the front door of his store, and then Tanner understood why Jacob was being so loud.

"I'm pleased to meet you all," Bethany said as she neared the women. "You can call me Bethany."

"My name is Samantha," said the tallest of the girls. She came forward and shook Bethany's hand. "These are my sisters."

"You all hungry?" Bethany asked. Tanner smiled, thinking how motherly Bethany could be sometimes. It was easy to see that these women were in need of some help.

"Yes please," Samantha replied. "We would appreciate it."

"Sheriff, can you help Tanner get the things I need from the store for Mrs. Roberts? And do let Mrs. Roberts know we'll have company for dinner and to plan a bigger menu. I'm going to take these women over to the laundry and help them get washed up," Bethany said, acting faster than Tanner could at that moment because he felt so stiff. He was sure proud of her willingness to help so quickly. "And Mr. Fry, please let Mrs. Fry know that I'll be back shortly for some new gowns for these women. They're going to need something a bit darker to work in."

"You hiring them?" Jacob asked as he placed his hands on his hips, baffled by it all.

"Well, I'm sure Matilda would. They were so great before that I think we can work something out," Bethany said with a smile. She then rounded up the women and led them down the road, leaving Tanner, Jacob, and Mr. Fry to watch in bewilderment.

"Now that you've let your woman put her hands into so many pies, she's just willing to jump right in, isn't she?" Jacob quipped as he came and sat down next to Tanner.

"I believe that Bethany had this side to her all along. She just never had the opportunity to do what she always wanted to, because she never knew what she wanted in life. I have thoroughly enjoyed watching her grow these last few weeks," Tanner replied.

"I was out doing my rounds, trying to find any sign of the women when I just came across them on the road. Had to come back to town to get the wagon, but I was just glad to see they were still alive. Seems they got lost trying to find the town," Jacob explained.

"Sheriff, would you mind explaining to me what just happened," Mr. Fry said, still a little baffled. "Weren't those the women that were working for the outlaws?"

"They were slaves, Mr. Fry," Jacob clarified. "They gave the outlaw leaders false information, and that is how we were able to defeat them so easily. We already knew how they were going to attack. Those women are really brave."

"Well, I'll be damned," Mr. Fry exclaimed. "I will go let the missus know that six women will be needing new gowns and that the town's new benefactor will be in to pay for them." Mr. Fry hurried inside then, and Tanner allowed himself to chuckle at it all.

"I don't think this town will ever be the same after what happened with these outlaws. The people are all working together, and it seems Bethany is making sure things get done around here so it can all be rebuilt," Tanner said, his heart full of love for the woman he would be marrying.

"And to think, it all started with an ad in a newspaper," Jacob said, rubbing his elbow into Tanner's shoulder.

"Well, let's get what the lady asked for. I know she was coming over here for some flour, and I better deliver that message to Mrs. Roberts. An extra six mouths to feed is a hefty order to fill," Tanner said as he did his best to push himself back onto his feet. Jacob was there in a moment to help him.

"I'm sure if Mrs. Tibet found out, she would be right over to help with the cooking," Jacob said as he led Tanner into the store.

"Did someone say cooking?" Mrs. Tibet said the moment they stepped into the store. They saw Mrs. and Mr. Tibet at the counter, making purchases of their own.

"Why yes, my dear. I sure did," Jacob said with a smile. Tanner could hardly believe all the luck he'd been having that day and knew this was a good sign of things to come.

CHAPTER 30

Bethany knew there had been a reason why she had stuffed the new wedding gown into her trunk the night she ran away from her father's house. And now, as she stood on the steps of the town hall, the building full of people gathered to see her married to Tanner, she understood why she had made that hasty decision. Though she had hated the idea of marrying Mr. Spark, the gown that had been quickly pinned for her was truly beautiful. She wore it with pride on the day of her actual wedding to the man she loved.

"Are you ready?" Jacob asked, holding her arm. She looked up at him and nodded, happy the sheriff was willing to walk her down the aisle. Together, they entered the town hall and started to make their way towards the front where Tanner was standing, a cane in his hand. Once those gathered noticed Bethany coming past the pews, the room quieted down and everyone stood to greet the bride.

"Who gives this woman to be this man's bride?" asked Pastor Munster once they reached the front.

"The sheriff of Bear Creek," Jacob said proudly. He placed Bethany's hand in Tanner's and gave the deputy a true stare, as if to warn Tanner away from being an improper husband. Tanner just smiled, and once Jacob had sat down with his own wife and daughter in the pew, the pastor began the ceremony.

Bethany faced Tanner and smiled up at him through her veil. She could hardly believe the day had come when she would finally get to marry the man she had fallen deeply in love with. Bethany knew that Tanner was a good man who would treat her well. She would be proud to create a family with him. He supported all her new endeavors in town, and even encouraged her working with the six sisters to establish Matilda's laundry business. In just one month, the new women of Bear Creek had all been settled and were doing much better. And the lumber mill was almost finished to start processing trees and getting the inn built once more.

Bethany was so focused on the wonderful moment of her wedding to Tanner that she didn't even notice that the town hall doors had opened. It was the sound of footsteps down the aisle that finally drew her attention from Tanner to those approaching. And when she saw a familiar man quickly approach her, she did her best to stifle the scream that rose up in her throat. Her father stood before her, and every part of her being was yelling at her to run.

"Bethany Duncan, you're coming home with me right now," her father said, his voice malicious. There were four armed men standing behind him, all of them with their pistols in their hands.

"I'd rather die than go anywhere with you," Bethany spat as she stepped closer to Tanner and wrapped her arms around him. Tanner placed his cane between Bethany and her father, and her father's eyes narrowed at the two of them.

Shuffling could be heard in the town hall as several men stood and drew their own pistols. Bethany looked around, noticing many familiar faces standing on her behalf and coming to her aid. With all the work she'd been doing at the laundry shop and the relief efforts she'd been trying to accomplish, she'd gotten to know quite a lot of people as the town was improved. The Sioux Indians that had also come to witness the marriage stood as well and started to slowly creep forward. She watched as her father's hired gunmen looked around and started to panic. One even holstered his pistol and started to back up towards the door. His friends seemed to notice his absence and soon turned and fled with the first, leaving her father all alone.

"If you don't come with me right now, I'll be completely ruined. You need to marry a wealthy man and save me from what Mr. Bradly has done to me," he shrieked. "First he steals from me and helps you escape. Next, he's trying to take over my business." Bethany was surprised to hear all of this. The fact that her father had blamed Mr. Bradly for everything helped her to feel a little bit relieved that at least he didn't realize that it was she who had stolen his money. She knew very well how much he had left in his safe and didn't feel bad for him one bit.

"Father, it's best if you leave this place or you're going to be in a world of hurt," Bethany said. "I never want to see you again and will never do a darn thing for you."

Mr. Duncan recoiled from Bethany's words, seeming to be shocked that his own flesh and blood would deny him. He started to look around then, seeing all the men surrounding him with their pistols drawn and the Indians with their daggers ready to defend the bride and groom. He looked once more at Bethany, his eyes wide with fright, before he dashed out of the town hall and towards the hired gunmen that had abandoned him.

It took a while for the congregation to settle once more. Bethany had her head bowed, her heart racing as she tried to rationalize what had just happened. Her father had found her after all, and yet she'd been able to stand up to him and not allow him to control her any longer. She could hardly believe this had happened all on her wedding day, but it seemed that she had finally conquered one of her worst fears. Telling her father no.

"Are you alright?" Tanner asked, his voice soft and gentle. Bethany nodded as she looked up at him through her veil.

"I wasn't expecting that," she admitted.

"I'm sure none of us were," Tanner replied, a smile on his face. "But you handled it well. He'll have to think twice about bothering you again. You've got an entire town willing to fight for you." That made Bethany truly smile, and as she took a deep breath, she was ready for the wedding ceremony to continue and officially come to the best part of the ending.

"Tanner Williams, do you take this woman to be your lawfully wedded wife?" asked Pastor Munster.

"I do," Tanner said confidently.

"And do you, Bethany Duncan, take this man to be your lawfully wedded husband?"

"I do," Bethany said in a happy and cheerful voice.

"Then by the power of God vested in me, I now pronounce you two Mr. and Mrs. Williams," came the booming voice of the pastor. The crowd erupted into applause, the sound deafening as Tanner used his good hand to fold back Bethany's veil and then lean forward to kiss her soundly on the lips. A bunch of people started whistling then, and Bethany couldn't help but smile as Tanner kissed her.

Since the weather was warm and the inn was under construction, there was a large potluck wedding celebration behind the town hall. Tables had been constructed to house all the food, while picnic blankets had been laid out on the lawn to give people a place to sit and eat. Bethany marveled at it all, the gathering of a whole town to celebrate one marriage, and the sheer amount of food that had been made and was currently being passed around.

"You know what the best part is about being married to you?" Bethany asked as she sat upon a blanket, her wedding gown spread out around her as she leaned against her husband.

"I'm going to have to guess it has something to do with my good looks," Tanner teased.

"No, silly," Bethany said as she chuckled. "It's waking up every morning by your side, knowing that no matter what life throws at us, we'll be able to handle it together. The best part is knowing that I will never be alone again in a home where I feel more like a bird in a cage, forced to sing but never free. You have given me more freedom in the last few months than I have ever felt in my entire life."

"And just look at how far you've flown, and the new heights you have reached," Tanner said in a proud voice, leaning towards her and kissing her on the lips. Bethany smiled once more, thinking that perhaps the best part of being married was enjoying the warm kisses that Tanner gave her.

EPILOGUE

There was a bitter chill to the wind as Bethany stood out on the front porch of the clinic. She'd just had a visit with Dr. Roberts to confirm that sometime in the spring she and Tanner would be expecting their first child. She was excited to head over to the sheriff's office and tell Tanner the good news before she went back to work at the laundry shop. With the weather turning cold, less people wanted to do their own laundry and hang it out back. They had put a wood-burning stove in the shop and hung clothes lines in the back so the clothes could be dried.

But what Bethany was looking at was the new foundation for the inn. All the rubble had been sifted through in case any of the Tibet's personal things could be salvaged from the fire. Very few things had survived, and it was a terrible loss for the older couple who had raised their children in that inn. Now, with the new foundation laid and the frame for the inn in place, Bethany could see that the inn was going to be twice as big as it once had been. And with the Tibet's children coming home for Christmas to witness the new building, it was sure to be a joyous celebration come the holidays.

Bethany tore her eyes from the construction of the building, feeling a sense of pride in her heart as she made her way over to the sheriff's office. She was glad that the money she'd stolen from her father was actually going towards a good cause. The lumber mill was fully functional now, situated north of town and managed by a bunch of strong Indian braves who had no issue manning the saw and processing the trees that they cut down. Everything seemed to be happening as planned. Including the large family that she wanted to have one day.

There was a smile on Bethany's face as she stepped into the sheriff's office and felt the warmth from the small wood stove in the corner. The sheriff was seated at his desk as he leaned forward, working hard on writing up his reports. The marshal needed all the details of what had happened in Bear Creek when the outlaws had threatened him, and Jacob had explained how he was trying to leave out the details about the six sisters so they wouldn't be bothered by the law. They'd already been through so much that it was time they were given the chance to live a normal life.

In fact, the six sisters had all gotten used to working at the laundry shop. They all shared the top apartment along with Matilda, and they seemed to grow happier with each passing day. They did everything together, from cooking to cleaning, to helping Matilda with the laundry business that earned them all some good money. Bethany truly hoped that they all would find the happiness in life that they deserved. And since no one, especially the men, had given them any trouble about women owning a business, Bethany was sure that one day soon they would all be able to settle down and have the type of families they'd dreamed about for so long.

"Hey there, good looking. You come in here for something?" Tanner teased as Bethany went over to his desk and sat on the corner, looking down at him with a bright smile.

"I just came by to see you," Bethany said, her smile growing by the second. She was so excited to tell Tanner the good news that she could hardly contain herself.

"Oh yeah? Any particular reason why?" he asked with a raised eyebrow. "Because a little birdie told me that you were going to go see a certain doctor today."

"Did Matilda tattle on me?" Bethany exclaimed, afraid her surprise had already been ruined.

"No," Tanner said with a chuckle. "I just happened to spot you heading that way when I was crossing the road to Fry's to see if any telegrams had come in for the sheriff."

Bethany sighed as she shook her head. "Should have known you would have heard the news from Fry's."

"So, what did Dr. Roberts say?" Tanner asked, seeming to be as excited as she felt.

"He confirmed that we will indeed be parents come the spring," Bethany enthused. Tanner was so happy that he quickly stood up and embraced Bethany. Jacob started clapping his hands as though it was a big celebration, and all Bethany could think to do was laugh openly. She was so happy that she could hardly contain how she felt. And to know that Tanner was also happy to become a parent made her feel reassured in all that they had accomplished together.

"Oh, I just can't wait to see this little baby!" Tanner said as he finally let Bethany go. "Hey, why don't we head out and let everyone know the good news."

"Don't you worry, they will find out soon enough. It's a small town, after all," Bethany said. "And I promised Morning Sun that I would come to camp today to learn how to make Indian stew. I'm going to take the wagon up, since I'm expecting."

"Good idea. You're not the best rider yet, anyways."

"No, but I am a pretty good driver," Bethany reasoned.

"Why don't the two of you go together?" Jacob suggested. "It's quiet around here, and all that's left are a bunch of reports. You two run along and tell the Chief I said hello. I'm sure he and Sandy will be having similar news soon as well. Their wedding wasn't that long ago, either."

"How exciting would that be?" Bethany said as Tanner got on his coat and hat.

"Well, let's head up to camp and go find out for ourselves," Tanner suggested as he opened the door for Bethany and bid the sheriff a good day. It was certainly hard to believe that Tanner was not afraid of Indians anymore. And with how the remote town of Bear Creek was starting to blossom and grow, Bethany was certain that their future together would continue to be full of even more unexpected and wonderful miracles.

The End

LIST OF CHARACTERS

- **Tanner Williams**
- **Bethany Duncan**
- Dr. Demetri & Emily Roberts
- Sandy Roberts
- Brown Bear, leader of the Sioux Indian camp
- Edward James & Morning Sun, Flying Jay
- Mr. Demetri Franklin, mayor of Bear Creek
- Dan & Phoebe Mavis
- Mathew & Jenny Jenkins, children: Michael (Mikey), Penelope,
- Louise & Margret Fritz, banker/ Jenny's mother
- Jacob & Rosa Benning, sheriff, children: Katelyn
- Peter Gibson, cattle hand
- Bobby Lukens, cattle hand
- Mr. & Mrs. Fry, dry goods owner, seamstress
- Pastor Barthelme Munster, traveling pastor

- Mr. & Mrs. Tibet, inn owners and local restaurant/café
- Curtis Denver, butcher
- Mitchel Franks, barber
- Varies ranchers, miners, homesteaders, and the local Sioux Indians

AMELIA'S OTHER BOOKS

Montana Westward Brides

#0 The Rancher's Fiery Bride

#1 The Reckless Doctor's Bride

#2 The Rancher's Unexpected Pregnant Bride

#3 The Lonesome Cowboy's Abducted Bride

#4 The Sheriff's Stubborn Secretive Bride

Bear Creek Brides

#1 The Rescued Bride's Savior

#2 A Faithful Bride For The Wounded Sheriff

#3 The Untangling of Two Hearts

#4 Indian Bride for the Trusty Miner

#5 Quick-Witted Bride for the Troubled Doctor

#6 A Loving Heart for the Loyal Deputy

CONNECT WITH AMELIA

Visit my website at **www.ameliarose.info** to view my other books and to sign up to my mailing list so that you are notified about my new releases and special offers.

ABOUT AMELIA ROSE

Amelia is a shameless romance addict with no intentions of ever kicking the habit. Growing up she dreamed of entertaining people and taking them on fantastical journeys with her acting abilities, until she came to the realization as a college sophomore that she had none to speak of. Another ten years would pass before she discovered a different means to accomplishing the same dream: writing stories of love and passion for addicts just like herself. Amelia has always loved romance stories and she tries to tie all the elements she likes about them into her writing.

Made in the USA
Middletown, DE
16 May 2022